"We did make this decision together, Liv," he reminded her.

"Uh-huh. I'm just not finding this platonic angle as easy to deal with as I thought it would be, that's all."

"And you think I am?" Grant pulled his chair closer and took her hands in his. "You think I'm enjoying not being able to make love to you? Do you know how many cold showers I've taken in the last week? How often I've been tempted to change the rules and just carry you off to some quiet inn for the weekend?"

"Would it be such a mistake to do that, Grant? The time for subterfuge ended the night we pledged to try to resurrect our relationship."

"Not 'relationship,' Olivia," he said. "What we're trying to revive is the love. So, yes, it would be a mistake. On the other hand…" He grinned, that devilish, disarming grin she'd never been able to resist. "I'm not made of stone…."

CATHERINE SPENCER, once an English teacher, fell into writing through eavesdropping on a conversation about Harlequin romances. Within two months she changed careers, and she sold her first book to Harlequin in 1984. She moved to Canada from England thirty years ago and lives in Vancouver. She is married to a Canadian and has four grown children—two daughters and two sons—plus a dog and a cat. In her spare time she plays the piano, collects antiques and grows tropical shrubs.

Catherine Spencer

THE MARRIAGE EXPERIMENT

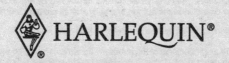

HARLEQUIN®

TORONTO • NEW YORK • LONDON
AMSTERDAM • PARIS • SYDNEY • HAMBURG
STOCKHOLM • ATHENS • TOKYO • MILAN • MADRID
PRAGUE • WARSAW • BUDAPEST • AUCKLAND

ISBN 0-373-18829-3

THE MARRIAGE EXPERIMENT

First North American Publication 2004.

www.eHarlequin.com

Printed in U.S.A.

CHAPTER ONE

GRANT saw Olivia before she noticed him. Or, more precisely, he saw her legs, because her face was hidden under the brim of a cream straw hat extravagantly ribboned in gold.

He'd have recognized those legs anywhere. Long and lusciously smooth as silk, they'd wrapped themselves around his waist too often for him not to know their every curve as intimately as he knew the back of his own hand.

Still, he was unprepared for his reaction to them again, all these years later. Arrhythmia was something he diagnosed in other people, not himself, and for his heart to behave so erratically at the sight of his ex-wife—or her limbs—was absurd. It wasn't as if he hadn't been expecting to see her, after all. He had come prepared.

She stood chatting with a guy who looked exactly like the kind of man her father would approve of. Nicely anemic and thoroughly tame. A ventriloquist's dummy, with Sam Whitfield no doubt literally putting the words into the poor guy's mouth.

Circling the tail-end of the receiving line, Grant waited until Olivia's date went off to refill her glass, then came up behind her and, just loudly enough for her to hear him over the buzz of other voices, murmured, ''Hello, sweet face.''

She reacted just as he'd hoped she would, spinning around so fast she almost fell out of her high-heeled pumps. "Grant?" she gasped, in a way that would have had him diagnosing respiratory distress if she'd been his patient.

"Olivia," he replied, working overtime to keep his own breathing under control. From a distance, she'd looked the same as always, but, up close, he saw that she'd changed.

It wasn't so much that she'd aged. She was still only twenty-eight—hardly in her dotage, after all. But her posture and the tilt of her head as she regarded him told him that not much remained of the eager, insecure girl he'd met and married eight years before. *She* would have looked at her feet and blushed. Fiddled with her hair or her pearls, and run her tongue nervously over her lower lip. But, recovering herself quickly, this latest model stared back at him as though daring him to blink in her direction.

Blink, hell! He stood there transfixed. She'd always had lovely eyes. Large and luminous, they were that particular shade of hazel able to switch from soulful brown to exotic green practically at will. But since he'd last seen her she'd learned to accentuate them with make-up. Not that she looked painted or anything, but someone had taught her to shape her brows into a more delicate arch, and to emphasize her long, fine lashes with mascara, so that the effect was not merely pretty but distractingly gorgeous. As for her mouth...

He tried to swallow inconspicuously, no easy feat given that his Adam's apple seemed to have swelled to the size of a watermelon.

Her mouth, he decided, looked like a freshly picked strawberry. Ripe and sweet and delicious. And he found himself remembering the first time he'd kissed her and how she'd tasted of summer and innocence. He couldn't have sworn to it, but he'd been pretty damned sure his was the first tongue to have slid past those lips and explored that naive mouth.

She obviously wasn't indulging in similar nostalgia. "How are you, Grant?" she said, her manner, like her voice, as polite and chilled as the French Chablis her father favored.

"Great," he croaked. "And you?"

"I'm…very well." Briefly, she pressed her lips together, the way women do when they've just put on fresh lipstick. "I'm surprised to see you here."

"Well, Justin and I go back a long way, further even than you and I. He wanted me here to help celebrate his wedding and I was happy to do whatever it took to make the day enjoyable."

"The way you enjoyed our wedding day?"

The irony in her tone caught Grant off-guard, flinging memories at him with such faithful attention to detail that he was forced to question how successful he'd been at closing the door on the past.

A simple garden wedding hadn't been good enough for Sam Whitfield's daughter. Hell, no! Nothing but a grandiose church affair would suffice, with the scent of gardenias and lilies suffocatingly heavy in the air.

The pews had been packed, mostly with strangers who'd lifted their noses in the air like a pack of suspicious pedigree dogs investigating the mongrel in their midst. Parked at the altar, Grant had stared at his face, grotesquely reflected in the shine of his new shoes, and wondered what the devil he was doing in that place, with those people, when there were so many other things he'd rather have been doing and so many ambitions remaining unfulfilled.

For one insane moment, he'd debated escaping while there was still time to call his life his own, but no sooner had the thought entered his mind than the organist had paused dramatically, then rolled full bore into Wagner's "Bridal March" when, in fact, "Send in the Clowns" might have been more appropriate.

Meeting Olivia's skeptical gaze now, he chose the most neutral reply he could come up with on short notice. "Our wedding was more formal."

"And you hated every minute of it."

"Yes," he said. "All those lilies reminded me of a funeral, but this…" He nodded at the scene around them: at the flower-decked arbor where the bride and groom had exchanged vows, at the swaying lilacs and the linen tablecloths lifting gently in the breeze, at the children racing up and down the lawns. Children had not been invited to the Whitfield-Madison nuptials for fear that they might disrupt things. "This I could have handled."

"Rubbish! You didn't want any kind of wedding, and especially not to me."

"Not true, Olivia," he said, picking his way through a minefield of truth to find an answer that would be acceptably cordial without compromising his integrity. "You were an unforgettably beautiful bride."

"And a disastrous wife. Don't bother denying it, Grant. We both know our marriage was a mistake. We didn't agree on a single thing."

"Your memory's either very short or very convenient," he said, surprised at how ticked off he was at the way she just shovelled their marriage aside as if it had been of no more consequence than a dust ball. "The sex was magnificent."

She almost blushed then. Just a hint of peach suffused her pale and flawless skin. But her gaze, like her voice, remained annoyingly steady. "You didn't need to marry me to have that, though, did you, Grant? You got that after just three dates."

"You make it sound as though I had my wicked way with a reluctant virgin, when we both know that wasn't the case. Virgin you undoubtedly were, honey, but the word 'reluctant' doesn't exactly spring to mind when I remember how eagerly you—"

"I was nineteen," she cut in, a tiny crack marring the surface of her polish at his crass reminder. "Young and innocent enough to believe that love and sex always went hand in hand and were strong enough to survive anything."

"Anything but your father," he said, snagging a couple of flutes of champagne from the tray of a passing waiter and handing one to her.

The edge in her voice could have sawn through steel when she replied, "Leave my father out of this, Grant."

"Pity you didn't feel that way eight years ago, Olivia," he said, tipping the rim of his glass against hers. "Perhaps if you had, instead of our standing here now exchanging trite unpleasantries, we'd be looking for a way to sneak off and enjoy a little afternoon delight."

The ventriloquist's dummy chose that moment to return, thus sparing Olivia having to weather more damage to her image as the perfectly-in-control divorcee facing off with her obnoxious ex. "Oh, I see someone already brought you another drink, Pussycat," he warbled, his pale blue eyes swinging from her heightened color and fixing themselves suspiciously on Grant. "I don't believe we've met. I'm Henry Colton, a very good friend of Olivia's."

It was a combination of things—her snotty hauteur, the man's proprietary attitude, the "pussycat" business—that stirred Grant to further mischief. "I'm Grant Madison, former lover and ex-husband of Olivia's."

"Grant!" Olivia sort of snuffled into her glass and aspirated on her champagne.

Relieving her of the drink, he thumped her gently between the shoulderblades and smiled affably at Henry Colton. "So tell me, Henry, exactly how do you define being a woman's 'very good friend'?"

"You don't have to answer that question, Henry," Olivia spluttered. "It happens to be none of Grant's business."

"It's all right, Olivia, I've got nothing to hide." Squaring his perfectly tailored shoulders, Henry stretched his neck as if he hoped that would bring his height up to six feet and put him more or less on a par with Grant's six-two. "We met at the bank. I'm the manager of Springdale Savings and Loan, you know—"

"I didn't know," Grant said. "Should I have?"

Olivia shot him a glance, part-pleading, part-loathing. "Please don't do this, Grant!"

"I'm merely being polite, sweet face," he said, massaging her shoulder soothingly. Her cream dress was sleeveless and held up by wide straps which dipped to a fetchingly low neckline. Even if he'd wanted to, he could hardly have avoided contact with her warm, smooth skin. "Go on, Henry. I'm fascinated."

Henry was fascinated, too—at the way Olivia's ex

was openly pawing her. Visibly trying not to stare at Grant's trespassing hand, he cleared his throat. "She sought me out when she was looking for sponsors for one of her fundraising efforts."

"Sought you out?" Grant tried to hide his snigger in a cough. Sam Whitfield deserved a medal for the job he'd done on this candidate!

Undaunted, Henry plowed on. "Neither of us was seeking a relationship at the time but..." He looked fixedly at the hand draped casually over Olivia's shoulder and a spark of something approaching outrage colored his voice. "How shall I put it to give you a clearer picture? There was a meeting of minds, as it were. We connected—strongly—and the rest, as they say, is history. We are an item. It's as simple as that."

The only simple thing around here is you, pal! Grant thought, unable to take the man seriously. "Funny how things happen sometimes, isn't it?" he said. "You think you've got life neatly figured out and, wham! In the blink of an eye, everything changes."

"When the right woman comes along, it's worth the upheaval," Henry declared so smugly Grant almost upchucked.

"And Olivia certainly knows how to generate upheaval," he said.

She didn't drive her high heel into his foot as she stepped past him but it wasn't for want of wishing she could. Talk about giving a guy the evil eye!

"Henry," she purred, sidling up to him and laying a manicured hand on his arm, "would you be a dear and get me a glass of water? Something around here is giving me a headache."

"Of course, Pussycat," he meowed back.

She watched as he wove a path among the other wedding guests, a small, serene smile on her face. "What a perfect ass you still are, Grant Madison," she cooed venomously.

"People don't change, Olivia," he said, wondering how long she could keep up with the china doll act, "no matter how hard others try to make them. I'd have thought it was a lesson too well learned for you to have forgotten it, considering how hard you tried—and failed—to shape me to fit your idea of what a husband should be."

"This might come as a crushing blow to your ego, Grant, but very little of the ten months we spent together is engraved on my memory. The seven years since have been more than enough time to erase you completely. That being the case, your harking back to our marriage is about as futile as sifting through cold ashes in the hope of stirring up a fire. Furthermore," she finished, giving her facial muscles a real work-out in order to preserve that phony smile, "you surely didn't come all the way back here just to dig up a past we both know is better left buried."

"You're right, sweet face. Autopsies never did hold much fascination for me. I'm far more interested in the living than the dead. So tell me, what's new with you since we parted company? Do you still live with Daddy? Does he monitor your every move? Is he grooming Henry to become the next Mrs. Olivia Whitfield? And is old Henry good in the sack?"

That wiped the smile off her face! "I have my own place, my own life and, as Henry already made perfectly clear, he and I are just friends," she spat, splashes of angry color flaring across her cheeks.

"You mean to tell me," he exclaimed, rearing back in feigned astonishment, "that he hasn't—that the pair of you don't—? Olivia, why the hell not? Can't he manage it? Because if that's a problem, there's treatment available that's rumored to be amazingly successful. Not that I've got personal knowledge, you understand, but I do keep up with the medical journals and—"

"Oh, shut up!" she practically wept, her composure collapsing like a house of cards. "Just shut up and go away!"

Since he'd been needling her precisely in the hope of stripping away all the lacquered perfection that made up this new Olivia Whitfield, success should have tasted sweet. Instead, it left a bitter taste on his tongue and filled him with a strange remorse. None of the things he'd thought he wanted—to have the last word, to be the one who walked away and left her standing—were nearly as tempting as the urge to wrap his arms around her and hold her close the way he had in the early days, when love was new and a kiss could work miracles.

Fortunately, a less welcome ghost from the past barreled onto the scene and put paid to any such nonsense. "So it is you," Sam Whitfield huffed, panting to a standstill in front of him and glaring at him from eyes embedded in too much florid flesh. "I was hoping I'd been mistaken. What persuaded you to slither back into town?"

"Same thing that brought you out from under your personal rock, Sam. Attending a wedding."

"Is that a fact? And how soon will you be leaving again?"

"Not for quite some time."

Sam assumed his familiar bulldog stance, legs planted a yard apart, jaw thrust forward pugnaciously. "I wouldn't have thought even you had the brass nerve to stay where you're so clearly not wanted. We've got a fine, well-staffed hospital here, and we don't need the likes of you hanging around, so take my advice, *Dr.* Madison, and go back to wherever it is you came from."

The chance to inflict a little torture on the man Grant despised above all others was too delicious to squander. Savoring every moment, he said, "But you do need me, at least for a while."

"What in the name of Hades are you talking about?"

"I'm standing in as Justin Greer's locum while he and Valerie are away on their honeymoon. I'm going to be in your face every day for the next two months, Sam, running his practice. Naturally, I assumed you already knew that, seeing you're chairman of the hospital board and a take-charge kind of guy."

Sam turned faintly purple. "You're delusional, Madison. I would never sanction any move that allowed you to cross the town limits, let alone set foot inside Springdale General again."

"Well, gee, Sam, then someone else must have okayed it when you weren't looking. Maybe you were on the ninth hole with your good buddy John Polsen at the time?"

It was a bone of contention that had lain buried for over eight summers, but it still raised Sam's hackles. Grant's internship hadn't been more than a month old when a freeway accident had swamped the emergency unit with casualties. One of them had happened to be John Polsen and, although his injuries hadn't been serious, Sam had pulled rank and had him bumped to the head of the line for treatment.

Brash, and as politically naive as they came, Grant had done what no one else had dared do: told the chairman of the board to stick to what he knew best—managing the hospital budget—and to leave the medical decisions to those who could recognize one end of a stethoscope from the other.

The fact that Sam had been indisputably in the wrong hadn't altered the fact that he'd been publicly humiliated by a lowly intern. The new Dr. Madison had needed to be taken down a peg or two, and Grant had known from then on that he didn't have a hope of serving his residency at Springdale. From that day forward, Sam had seen to it that Grant always wound up at the end of whatever line he chose to stand in.

Rubbing the man's nose in the fact that he'd been out-maneuvered yet again by his old upstart of an enemy gave Grant a special kind of satisfaction now. In his view, no amount of punishment he could dole out would ever even the score between him and Olivia's father. The bitterness ran too deep. On both sides.

"Even with the ink on your diploma barely dry you were an arrogant bastard, and nothing's changed, obviously," Sam growled. "It's no thanks to you that John Polsen didn't die, the day they brought him into Emergency."

"Bull, Sam!" Grant said cheerfully. "John Polsen's like you—too mean to die."

"Stop it, both of you!" Olivia begged, observing the old warhorse fearfully. "For heaven's sake, Grant, can't you see my father isn't a well man? This kind of strain is bad for his heart."

Too many sixteen-ounce steaks, after-dinner ports and foot-long cigars are the real culprit in that department, Grant could have told her. But there was a limit to everyone's tolerance for stress and Olivia had clearly reached hers. Her eyes were dark with worry and she slipped her arm part-way around the old man's girth as tenderly as a mother. "Don't upset yourself," she told him soothingly. "It isn't worth it. *He* isn't worth it."

"Maybe you should find him a seat in the shade," Grant offered, a little alarmed himself at Sam's stertorous breathing and the sweat suddenly popping out on his brow.

The glare she flung at him would have stopped traffic. "I hardly need you to tell me how to take care of my father. In fact, given the circumstances, you're the last person I'd turn to for advice."

"Suit yourself." He shrugged and inclined his head at the crowd lined up at a buffet groaning under the weight of lobster mayonnaise, cracked Dungeness crab, prawns in aspic, smoked turkey and roast beef. "But you'd be doing him a favor if you steered him away from all that rich food."

Not deigning to acknowledge what she surely knew was a sound recommendation, she carted Sam off to a table set in the shade of a grand old oak, and plunked him down in a chair. Shortly after, Henry Colton joined them. What a sight they made, with him fawning all over the old man and practically drooling on her, Sam sitting there like a king holding court, and Olivia, the ever-dutiful daughter, anticipating her father's every need and waiting on him hand and foot.

Collaring Justin, who happened to stroll past at that

moment, Grant nodded at the trio. "Do you see anything wrong with that picture?"

Justin didn't miss a beat. "Apart from the fact that you're no longer in it, you mean?"

Grant snorted and muttered a satisfyingly obscene expletive. "I hardly think I've been missed! But there's something sadly lacking in a twenty-eight-year-old woman whose idea of high living is to act as handmaiden to her tyrant of a father."

"Yeah." Justin nodded. "So what do you propose to do about it, pal?"

"Me?" Grant grimaced. "Not a blasted thing!"

"Why not? Isn't that why you really came back to Springdale?"

Incensed, he snapped, "You know very well it's not!"

But Justin was no more the type to back away from a scrap than Grant himself was. "Come off it, Grant! I agree you're doing me a favor by covering my practice while I'm away, but would you have been so eager to stand in if it were anyone else—or, more to the point, any*where* else? Admit it, you've got another, less altruistic reason for being here. So what's on that private agenda of yours? Going another ten rounds with Sam Whitfield for the sheer hell of it— or trying once more to wean Olivia away from him?"

An hour ago, Grant could truthfully have declared Sam the hands-down winner. That the situation had changed, however, wasn't something he was prepared to admit to anyone. Deeming ambiguity the better part of discretion, he merely grinned at Justin and raised his glass in a mocking toast. "Let's just drink to marriage, pal," he said. "May the honeymoon never end."

* * *

Up to her neck in bubbles, Olivia lay back in the soaker tub, rested her head against the inflatable pillow, and wallowed in the scented warmth of the water. Gradually, the tension seeped out of her limbs, eased away by a languor that crept along her shoulders and up the back of her neck. Only when a slight ache swept the length of her jaw did she realize she'd been clenching her teeth for longer than was good for her, or them.

Of course, she knew why she'd been coiled tight as a spring. She'd behaved like a complete idiot at the wedding. By now, everyone else in town probably knew it, as well. And the reason could be succinctly summed up in two words: Grant Madison.

To say that she'd gone into shock at first sight of him scarcely began to describe the jolt to her system. Her father wasn't the only one who'd run the risk of cardiac arrest. She'd felt pretty close to it herself, the way her heart had literally thundered to a stop before resuming an erratic rhythm and banging wildly against her ribs. But that was nothing compared to what had happened later, after the sun had gone down behind the hills and left the garden dappled in purple shadows.

By then, she'd begun to recover from the trauma of coming face to face with her ex-husband, even to relax a little, which was never a good idea around Grant. But he'd seemed more than happy to keep his distance, and when Henry had asked her to dance, she'd accepted. There'd been no reason not to. He was a good, if conservative, dancer, just about all the other guests had been up on their feet, and what better way to celebrate the wedding of two well-known, well-respected Springdale residents than in a turn around the dance floor imported for the occasion?

People had already been talking, of course, even then. Those who'd known Grant in the past hadn't forgotten him, or his stormy marriage to the chairman of the hospital board's daughter, and they'd been more than willing to supply the details to those meeting him for the first time. She'd have had to be both blind and stupid not to have noticed the sly glances directed at her, or the way conversation had suddenly stopped whenever she'd come within earshot. If upstaging the bride and groom had been his intent, Grant had succeeded in spectacular fashion.

But Olivia had come a long way since she'd watched him walk out on their marriage. In the seven years since, she'd grown up, and no longer hid behind the high stone walls of her father's house. So she'd held her head high and smiled determinedly as Henry had swept her around the floor in a precisely correct fox-trot.

If only the music hadn't changed...if only Henry didn't feel that jive was something best reserved for leather-clad delinquents....

Sighing, she reached for the loofah and scrubbed languidly at her right leg. *If only she'd had the good sense to say no!* But Grant had caught her off-guard, stepping in the moment Henry had released her and grasping her by both hands. ''Care to show 'em how it's done, sweet face?'' he murmured.

''I really must protest,'' Henry began.

''Must you really?'' Grant replied with a grin. ''And how do you propose to do that, Henry, old sport? Knock my block off?''

Even if he'd been so inclined, at five-ten and only a hundred and seventy pounds or so, Henry was no match for a man of Grant's build. Comparing the two, Olivia experienced a shocking sense of *déjà vu* as she recalled the first time she'd seen Grant without any clothes.

Doctors weren't supposed to be so broad-shouldered or narrow-waisted. They usually weren't blessed with muscular arms, long, athletic legs, and a chest tailor-made to take a woman's breath away. They were supposed to be studious and serious and kind and safe and, like Henry, a little bit stooped around the shoulders. And what an M.D. looked like stark naked wasn't supposed to be the first thing a woman thought about when confronted by him.

Henry, bless his soul, didn't have a clue about what she was thinking. "Olivia? Do you want me to get rid of this fellow?"

"It's all right, Henry," she said, aware that she was mesmerized by Grant's laughing blue eyes and even more shamefully aware of the sudden rush of moist electric heat dampening her underwear. "I can handle this myself. If Dr. Madison would like to dance, I'm willing to accommodate him."

Accommodate him, indeed! And far more intimately than Henry could begin to guess! Consigning self-preservation to another time, she let Grant draw her into the seething, insistent tempo of "Proud Mary", and as if it had been only yesterday, they rediscovered the wordless affinity of two people who knew one another so well that their bodies instinctively interacted as one.

How was it possible for a dance to be so charged with vibrant energy and yet to smolder with such sultry tension? Half the time he sent her spinning away from him, with nothing but the sure grip of his fingers to anchor her. And she let herself go, confident that he wouldn't lose her, that she wouldn't stumble, that, eventually, he'd bring her back to him. As he did, drawing her hard and close to him so that their thighs locked and their hips rocked in grinding, hypnotic motion.

Then, when she thought she could bear it no longer and was sure everyone around them knew she was melting for him, he'd fling her away again, turn her so that her spine rubbed against his chest, pass his hand around his waist and offer it behind his back so that, as she swung by him, her arm brushed against him and her fingers wanted dreadfully to drift down and linger on the taut curve of his buttocks.

Oh, he was a devil in disguise, no doubt about it, and she a mindless fool for not putting an end to matters when she had the chance! But, too dazzled to sense the danger, she remained with him and let him draw her into the next dance, a slow, slow number which invited—no, which *guaranteed* intimacy and full body contact—and he crooned softly in her ear *This Guy's In Love*. Words to break her heart, because he'd never really been in love with her.

To hide the sudden pang of regret which blurred her vision, she closed her eyes and dropped her head to his shoulder. He gave a little growl of satisfaction and, folding her hand against his heart, tilted his hips so that she couldn't possibly miss noticing how thoroughly aroused he was. Which was what it always came back to, with Grant. Sex, sex, and sex. As if that was enough to make her forget the hurt and betrayal he'd dealt out to her.

So, to let him know that she wasn't about to be seduced again, she reared back and practically shrieked, "How dare you, Grant Madison?"

"Well," he muttered, obviously chagrined, "it's not as if I took the damned thing to obedience school and had it trained to perform on command! When a woman presses her nice soft body up against a man, he's likely to react."

Too late, she realized that the music had stopped. Had the people closest overheard the exchange? she wondered, appalled. Were the titters and giggles and one or two outright guffaws directed at her, or were they just the normal reactions of people enjoying a wedding party?

Surely they were. But did she comport herself with dignity, as befitting a woman of her position in the community, and simply walk away from Grant Madison and his deplorable behavior? Oh, no, not Olivia Margaret Whitfield! As if they hadn't already put on enough of a floor show, she hauled off and slapped him across the cheek as a grand finale.

Groaning at the recollection, she drew in a long breath and submerged her head beneath the water, wishing she could drown herself. How would she ever face people again, after such a performance? Worse still, how would she face him, as she'd undoubtedly have to do if, as he'd claimed, he'd be acting as Justin Greer's locum for the next two months?

CHAPTER TWO

For the next two days, Olivia literally hid from the world. Turning off her phone, she buried herself in tasks about the gatehouse, spending Sunday morning painting the powder room at the back of the hall, and the afternoon weeding the flower garden bordering the patio.

On Monday, thanks to the miracle of modern computers, she was able to put in a full day's work without once stepping outside her front door. But when she found herself actually planning to lie about not feeling well rather than attend a scheduled meeting at Springdale General on the Tuesday, she knew the self-indulgence had gone on long enough.

"Grow up, Olivia!" she muttered. "After Saturday's wedding debacle, showing your face in public again won't be easy, but you've survived worse."

An hour later, she wasn't sure that was true.

"Hear your husband's back in town," Ingrid from the deli greeted her, when she stopped by on her way to the hospital. "Hear your father's fit to be tied about it, too."

There wasn't much Ingrid didn't hear in the course of a week. The little tea shop at the back of her premises was well patronized by local matrons and a hive of gossip, even when there was nothing much to talk about. The return of the renegade Dr. Madison would have made front page news even if he'd come sneaking into town under a cover of darkness. Olivia wasn't the only one who'd found his slow, sexy smile and hypnotically persuasive voice irresistible.

"I'll take a jar of black olives, please, and a small carton of the bean salad," she said stiffly, hoping to nip the conversation in the bud. "And, just for the record, he's my ex-husband."

But picking up subtle hints never had been one of Ingrid's strong points. "Don't think folks haven't noticed, hon! There's a whole flurry of social events suddenly being planned and, as usual, the first one out of the gate is Mrs. Bowles. Just yesterday, she booked me to cater a garden party and let slip that Dr. Madison's name's at the top of her list of invitees. And I guess we all know why." She weighed the salad, slapped a lid on it, and hitched her bosom on the edge of the glass-fronted display case of imported cheeses, a sure sign she was settling in for the duration. "She didn't shell out the better part of eight thousand dollars to make her daughter presentable just to have her sitting home and withering on the vine, as it were. Now that Joanne's got the braces off her teeth and shed all that extra weight, Mrs. Bowles is looking to fix her up with a rich husband. And if the car your ex is driving is anything to go by, he's not exactly on the bread line."

"I'm afraid I can't comment on that, since I have absolutely no idea what sort of car he's driving, nor any interest in finding out."

"No," Ingrid said slyly. "I guess you've been too busy checking out his other assets. Having second thoughts about the divorce, are you?"

"Certainly not!"

"Probably just as well. From all I've heard, he's a bit more than a woman like you can handle."

The way Ingrid looked at her, she might have been the offspring of a troll trying to pass for human.

"Thank you very much!" Olivia said, and made her escape. But, instead of heading directly to the hospital, she detoured by way of the park and found a bench in a quiet corner overlooking the river. She needed a few moments to collect herself before running the risk of facing anyone else because, in her present state, she could only be described as a mess.

Why had Ingrid's last comment hurt so much when it coincided exactly with the conclusion she herself had arrived at years ago? Why did it matter that every eligible woman within hailing distance was setting her sights on Grant Madison, or that invitations were being issued and she probably wouldn't be receiving any? And why couldn't she forget how it had felt to be in his arms again, to feel his heart beating beneath her hand?

She knew the answer and it had nothing to do with falling in love again—at least, not with him. It had to do with his all-too-accurate assessment of her relationship with Henry.

She was a woman in her prime. She should be married and pregnant, with one or two children already hanging onto her skirts. She should have a warm, exciting body sleeping next to her in bed each night.

Instead, she had Henry, who'd implied more than once that he was in love with her. But the thought of actually *making* love with him left her cold, and he fortunately was too much the gentleman to press the point. Unlike Grant....

Unbidden, the memories of that long-ago summer

came sweeping back. She'd been just two months shy of her twentieth birthday when they'd met, and to say that she'd fallen in love with the handsome new intern was an absurd understatement. She'd literally tumbled headlong into a passion so hot and intense it had nearly killed her.

On their third date, Grant had rented a boat and they'd spent the afternoon drifting down the river. Because of the heat, she'd worn a white sun dress with nothing underneath but a pair of cotton panties, and he'd worn denim cut-offs and a blue golf shirt. Spreading out her skirt, she'd reclined against the boat cushions, rested her head against one raised arm, and let the fingers of her other hand trail through the water, all the time watching him through half-closed eyes, admiring the play of muscles beneath the smooth tanned skin of his arms and legs, and very much aware that he was watching her.

A few miles past the town limits, he'd steered into a quiet backwater, tethered the boat, and led her up the bank toward a huge old weeping willow. She'd sensed the urgency in him, had seen the smoldering passion in his eyes. When he'd drawn her down beside him in the long, sweet grass, she'd known he wasn't going to stop at a kiss or two, just as she'd known she wasn't going to object at his wanting more from her.

Even all these years later, remembering made her blush. How willingly she'd sprawled beside him, with her skirt up around her waist and the straps of her dress pulled down to reveal her breasts, and her underwear hanging off one ankle! How brazenly she'd let him pleasure her, moaning low in her throat as he'd skimmed his lips over the slope of her shoulder and at excruciating leisure taken each pebbled nipple in his mouth! And how trustingly she'd opened to him, her flesh so slick and eager and his so hard and hot and big that the pain as he'd entered her had barely had time to register before it had been thrust aside by raging passion.

Today, the sun shot brilliant silver arrows through her closed eyelids, but that day the light had been the softly diffused green of a tranquil, underwater sort of world. After the loving, she'd lain there for the longest time, waiting for him to say the right words, the *only* words a woman wants to hear when she's given herself unconditionally to a man.

Instead, the silence had lengthened and left her wondering if he'd found her a terrible disappointment. When she'd finally found the courage to look at him, he'd been stretched beside her with his head propped up on his hand and a lazy smile on his face. "Hey," he'd murmured.

Hey, what? she'd almost cried. *What does that mean? And what happens next?*

What had happened next was that he'd climbed back into his cut-offs as casually as though he was quite used to baring his all in the great outdoors and, glancing at his watch, reached down and hauled her to her feet. "We'd better head back," he'd said, planting a swift kiss on her mouth. "I'm due at the hospital in another hour."

There'd been grass stains on her dress, and she'd cried all the way home as aftermath had set in. "Everyone will know what we've done," she'd wailed.

"How?" he'd said. "I'm not planning on spreading the news."

"They'll be able to tell, just by looking at me!"

He'd bent over the oars and grinned in that carefree way of his. "You don't look any different to me, sweet face," he'd said.

She'd been devastated. How could he appear so untouched by what they'd shared, when she would never again be the same?

Her father had sensed the change in her immediately, and when Grant hadn't phoned the next day, as promised, had said cryptically, "That's what you get for giving in to a man like Madison. He's using you, Olivia, and you'll live to regret the day you met him."

True enough, she thought now, dashing impatiently at the tears suddenly stabbing at her eyes. And if she was so determined to revive the past, she'd do well to dig up some less romantic memories, such as the day she'd told him she was pregnant, in the February following their September wedding.

"Oh, damn!" he'd sighed, sinking to the edge of their bed and lowering his head into his hands. "How the hell did that happen?"

As if he hadn't known!

Better yet, what about the day he learned she'd miscarried? "A blessing in disguise," he'd said, using his most professional bedside manner. "I know you're hurting now, but you're young and healthy and there's no reason you can't carry a baby to term when the time's right. But that time, Olivia, is not now."

Of course it hadn't been—at least, not for someone who'd secretly applied to work on a medevac team in the Northwest Territories once his year of internship was up, and who, if he was accepted, would spend at least half his time away from home. But that was the kind of man she'd married—too focused on his own wants and needs to give a hoot about anyone else's, least of all a wife who'd become a millstone around his neck.

The bitter after-taste of that long-ago time acted like a tonic on her wilting spirits. No longer just Sam Whitfield's daughter or Dr. Grant Madison's wife, she was a woman of consequence in her own right and deserving of the respect she'd earned. No one had the power to reduce her life to a shambles, and she would not give credence to the gossip currently circulating by hiding herself away.

Brushing a speck of dirt from the sleeve of her jacket, she rose from the bench and walked purposefully through the park gates and across the road to the main entrance of the hospital.

At that hour of the morning, the main lobby was crowded with visitors, clerks, technicians and other medical personnel, all busily going about their business. Yet more than a few curious gazes followed her as she made her way to the bank of elevators, and Olivia knew that the gossip hadn't stopped at Ingrid's Deli. The hospital was buzzing, too, and if she'd had the slightest doubt of that, it was laid to rest the minute she stepped into the boardroom where her meeting was to take place.

"So you haven't holed up in your little house for the duration," Daphne Jerome, head of the social committee, greeted her. "My dear, how I do admire your fortitude!"

Since Daphne didn't admire anyone but herself, her remark could be construed as nothing more than a blatant attempt to get an account, from the source, of what had actually happened on the Saturday. Feigning surprise, Olivia said blandly, "I don't know what you're talking about, Daphne."

"Why, the reappearance of your unlamented ex-husband, of course! From all accounts, he quite stole the limelight at Justin Greer's wedding—and you didn't do so badly, yourself. How did it feel to come face to face with him after all this time?"

"Not particularly exciting. We've been divorced for so long, it was almost like meeting a stranger."

"Really? In that case, I shudder to think how you'd greet a friend."

Realizing too late the mistake of trying to play Daphne at her own game, Olivia said shortly, "A woman your age ought to know better than to set much store by hearsay, and I frankly don't have the time to waste setting you straight. Where's Dr. Harte? I thought that, as head of Cardiology, he wanted to sit in on today's meeting."

"Haven't you heard? He's been called out of town. And since his next-in-command is Dr. Greer, who happens to be off on his honeymoon, that leaves only *his* stand-in, and…" Daphne smiled archly. "Well, dear, I see from the look on your face that you're beginning to get the picture—and just in time, because here he is, in the flesh."

The small silence which punctuated her announcement probably lasted no longer than a heartbeat, yet it seemed to Olivia that it stretched interminably, during which time everything happened in slow motion.

Grant closed the door and confronted the faces turned expectantly to his. Sparing the room at large a brief, professional smile, he nodded a reply to the murmured greetings and favored her with a pleasant,

"Morning, Olivia," as he took the chair Daphne indicated was his.

Olivia wasn't quite sure how she found her place, but the relief at being able to sit down before her knees gave way was overwhelming. How had Saturday's outrageous and irreverent dancing partner metamorphosed into this white-coated stranger with the cool blue eyes and air of distinguished respectability? What had happened to the rebel in blue jeans who'd once stalked the halls of Springdale General and thumbed his nose at those in authority whom he perceived to be fools—most notably her father?

Blindly, she reached into her briefcase for her folder of notes, and wondered what other surprises Grant had hidden up his immaculately starched sleeve. Under cover of uncapping her pen, she sneaked another look at him, half expecting to find him laughing at her for being taken in by so ludicrous a performance. Because surely that was all it was?

But, if so, he wasn't ready to put an end to it. Instead, he sat listening attentively to the man on his right, nodding occasionally in a serious sort of way and absently polishing a pair of rimless glasses. *Add a false beard,* Olivia thought, more confounded by the minute, *and he'd pass for a college professor!*

Someone called the meeting to order and droned on about various administrative concerns. The minutes from the last meeting were read, during which Grant seemed to find staring out of the window vastly more interesting than paying attention to the proceedings.

The social committee's fundraising efforts came fifth on the agenda, and when, finally, they were opened for discussion, Daphne took the floor. "I'd like to begin by introducing Dr. Grant Madison, who's here specifically to enlist our support for the Cardiac Unit. Before we get down to specifics, I'll ask those of you involved in this particular undertaking to identify yourselves, just so that he knows who you are. We'll start with you, Ms. Whitfield.''

And say what? *Hello, I'm your ex-wife, who hasn't been able to get you off her mind since you marched back into her life three days ago and practically seduced her in front of half the town?* Though truthful, such an admission was hardly appropriate.

Olivia's dismay must have been painted on her face, because Grant cut in before she could open her mouth. ''No introduction's needed. Olivia and I are already well acquainted.''

A titter rippled around the table at that, but soon died when he continued sharply, ''And, since I'm sure your time is as valuable as mine, I suggest we forego the social niceties and cut to the chase.''

He scanned the table at large, and although his gaze this time settled on her only briefly, Olivia thought she detected a sympathetic gleam in his eyes. ''At your last meeting, Dr. Harte made clear the dire need for new equipment in CCU. You waived making a decision on whether or not to support his request for help in raising the funds required until you'd had time to study the feasibility of such an undertaking. I'm here now as his representative to find out your answer.''

Such a direct approach allowed for little equivocation on the part of the committee, particularly not with his unblinking stare dissecting every face as decisively as a laser beam. Even Daphne squirmed a little, and couldn't wait to pass the buck elsewhere.

"You're the one who's done the research on this, Olivia," she said. "Are we going to be able to assist, and if so, how?"

"We've already pledged support to other departments," she began, wondering how she'd managed to make her voice sound so calmly confident when her insides were in a total uproar. "And I recommend that we honor those first, but—"

"Which departments, Olivia?" Grant inquired.

"Maternity and the Outpatient Clinic, for a start, but—"

"Their situations aren't as critical."

"No, they aren't. But under the circumstances, I feel that—"

"How you feel isn't the issue," he said tersely. "We're talking about saving lives here. With all due respect, childbirth is a normal function which the female body is superbly designed to deal with, and most deliveries are free of complications—"

"But not all of them, Dr. Madison," she cut in, any inclination she might have harbored to view him in a more kindly light fast disappearing. "Although you can be forgiven for having forgotten that, since it's never been an area of particular interest to you."

For a second or two they locked gazes, and she knew from the faint flush that ran under his skin that he recognized the private condemnation behind her remark. But he recovered quickly and overrode it so thoroughly she might as well have saved herself the bother of airing it. "I don't wish to be offensive, but you're scarcely qualified to determine priorities here. The Outpatient Clinic, by definition, is not an acute care facility. Anyone requiring round-the-clock supervision would be admitted to one of the wards."

She laid down her pen and said very distinctly, "I know."

"I don't think you do, since you're clearly unable to view the matter with any kind of objectivity. You need to consult an expert before you—"

"Dr. Madison," she interrupted, taking great pleasure in cutting him off for a change, "I don't presume to tell you how to do your job. I'd appreciate it if you'd afford me the same professional courtesy and not try telling me how to do mine. Now, if I may continue?"

He gave a condescending little smile, as though she were a child he had to humor. "Please do."

She could have choked him! "Thank you so much!"

"You're welcome."

Aaagh! Fairly spitting out the words, she went on, "I have completed an exhaustive study of the various proposals put forward by the members of this committee, and it is my recommendation that we divert existing funds to those departments who've already appealed to us for help. That would leave us free to direct the proceeds of our next major fundraiser to the Cardiac Unit."

"Would it, indeed?" he said, in a somewhat more deferential tone. "I see."

But she was in no mood to be conciliatory when he'd done his best to belittle her in front of her colleagues. "You'd have seen a lot sooner if you'd had the good manners to let me finish a sentence without interruption."

"I stand corrected," he said, bathing her in his most charming smile. "Would it be out of line for me to ask how soon this major fundraising event will take place?''

''In August,'' she snapped, aware that no one was missing a syllable of their exchange and that to continue the battle of one-upmanship was not only likely to end in defeat for her, but would also add to the gossip already circulating. ''At the hospital's annual carnival.''

''Carnival…? Oh, of course, that day-long shindig culminating in the Sunflower Ball! How could I have forgotten?''

How indeed, since the only one he'd attended had been during those hungry pre-wedding days when they hadn't been able to get enough of each other, and, while everyone else had been sipping wine between waltzes, he'd whisked her out from under her father's nose and spent most of the evening making love to her in the rose arbor at the Country Club!

''Very easily, I'm sure,'' she said, stuffing her papers into her briefcase as everyone else began drifting toward the coffee urn set up on a trolley at the far end of the room. ''But if you care to have your memory refreshed…'' she indicated Daphne, hovering expectantly well within earshot ''…speak to Mrs. Jerome, here. She chairs the social end of things and I don't doubt she'd be delighted to fill you in on the details. Now, if you'll excuse me…''

Dismissing him with a nod, she slid a sheet of paper across the table to Daphne. ''Here's a list of our latest sponsors, which I'll leave for you to present to the others when the meeting reconvenes. If any other names come up, you can let me know later.''

''Aren't you staying for coffee, dear?''

''Not today. I have another meeting to attend.''

"I'll walk you out," Grant said.

Plainly disappointed that the circus was over for the day, Daphne said, "What a pity you both have to leave, just when we're about to take a social break. But I suppose you'd prefer to be alone to catch up on each other's doings?"

"Not at all," Olivia said stonily. "Dr. Madison and I no longer share anything in common, at least not on a personal level, so by all means feel free to enjoy his company."

Deciding that was about as good an exit line as she could come up with, she made a beeline for the door.

He wasn't about to be shaken off so easily, however. She'd barely left the room before he came striding out after her. "Just a minute, Olivia. You and I need to get a few things straight."

But she'd had enough for one day, and when she saw the green arrow light up above the polished brass doors of the elevator at the end of the hall, she seized her chance to escape another lecture.

"Some other time, Doctor," she said breezily, and, sprinting forward, managed to squeeze into the crowded car just before the doors slid shut in his face.

That afternoon, the temperature shot up into the low nineties. Not even the breeze off the river was enough to stir the air, and by the time Olivia got home, shortly after five, her smart linen suit was clinging to her like warm, limp lettuce.

Dropping her briefcase on the hall table, she propped open both front and back doors, flung wide all the windows, and hauled herself upstairs, intent on stripping down to the barest essentials and submersing herself in her swimming pool with all due speed.

Add a little background music, a glass of cold white wine, and nothing but the fragrance of the heliotrope growing in pots around her patio to disturb the peace, and perhaps she'd begin to unwind from a day which had never quite recovered from the encounter with Grant.

Stupid, she knew, to let him get under her skin like that, but the way he'd behaved at the meeting had floored her. Though always something of a maverick, the young intern she'd once known and fallen in love with had been the least pretentious man she'd ever met, and had borne no resemblance at all to this morning's arrogant nitpicker.

But the memory of his remarks, the scornful tone of his voice, his patronizing smile and confident assumption that she'd jump on command if he ordered her to, continued to mock her, even after she'd swum several lengths of the pool and collapsed on a chaise in the shade of a large sun umbrella.

You're scarcely qualified to determine priorities...you're clearly unable to view the matter with any kind of objectivity...you need to consult an expert....

"The nerve of him, condescending to me like that, as if I were still the wet-behind-the-ears girl he married!" she muttered indignantly, taking a swig of her wine.

A second later, the glass all but slipped from her fingers as a familiar voice inquired, "Do you often get plastered and start talking to yourself, sweet face? Because if you do, you should be aware that it's a very dangerous habit to adopt which can and usually does lead to serious and long-lasting consequences."

CHAPTER THREE

LOOKING supremely at ease, and for all the world as if he had every right to be there, he lounged against the frame of the French doors leading from her living room, his shabby attempt to look grave sadly undermined by the supercilious little smirk on his face.

"How did you get in here, Grant?" she spat, doing her best to sound both dignified and affronted—no easy task given that she was sprawled out practically naked before him and he was making no secret of the fact that he'd noticed.

"I let myself in," he said, staring his fill at great leisure. "The butler doesn't seem to be on duty. I thought perhaps you'd given him the night off."

"I don't have a butler."

His smirk grew. "What, and no maid, either? Gee, it must be tough, having to do for yourself!"

"It is. But somehow I manage." Aware that her strapless bikini top was precariously close to letting all it was supposed to contain fall out before his amused inspection, she tried rather unsuccessfully to cover herself with a towel.

Of course, if he'd had a grain of decency in his make-up, he'd have averted his eyes and let her fumble in private, but he'd never been long on chivalry. "You don't seem to be managing that too well," he drawled, shoving himself away from the door frame and ambling toward her. "Need any help?"

"Not from you," she fumed, slapping the towel in his direction to keep him at a distance.

"No need to get all exercised, Olivia," he said mildly. "I didn't come here with seduction in mind."

"What did you come for, then?" To her horror, the question emerged loaded with unintentional petulance, a fact he was also quick to pick up on.

"You sound almost disappointed, sweet face, as if it's been a long time since a man reminded you how it feels to respond like a woman. Am I to take it that Hank from the Bank is no great shakes between the sheets?"

"His name is Henry," she exclaimed, almost choking with anger, "and I thought I made it plain on Saturday that we are not lovers! This might come as a surprise to you, Grant, but there are men for whom sex is not the be-all and end-all of existence."

"Only if they've been neutered." Uninvited, Grant took a turn around the patio, peering into the various jardinieres as if he suspected Henry might be lurking amid the flowers. "If you were my woman, I'd be out defending my territory, especially if her unattached ex suddenly showed up in town."

"But I'm not *your* woman. I never was, although I suppose it would be expecting too much for you to understand the difference between sharing your life with someone and treating her as if she were just another possession to load in the trunk of your car."

"I was willing to share my life with you, Olivia," he said, the very softness in his tone a warning as lethal as a jungle cat's low snarl. By now, the sun had begun its descent toward the horizon so that his shadow lay long and narrow on the flagstones, making it seem almost as if he were reaching out to her.

"I was willing to share everything—all my dreams and ambitions and, most assuredly, my heart. You just weren't interested in coming along for the ride."

His accusation brought the resentment she'd thought she'd buried years before rising up to engulf her, along with a smattering of remembered agony and a wealth of bitterness. "You're the one who walked out, Grant Madison, not I, so don't try re-writing history now, because I'm not about to buy it! I might not have been bright enough to have the letters 'M.D.' after my name, but I was far from the simpleton you took me to be. I knew exactly what you were doing, the day you presented me with an ultimatum no sane person would have found accept-able. You wanted an excuse to back out of our mar-riage and you found one."

"I offered you adventure and freedom," he said, the sudden edge in his voice sharp as a scalpel, "but you didn't have the guts to seize opportunity when it came knocking. Instead you chose to remain in your father's shadow and to hell with me!"

"As if you even cared! Your only passion was medicine."

"Not just medicine, Olivia. At one time, I was pas-sionate about you, too."

"You didn't let that stop you from abandoning me at a time when I was most vulnerable, though, did you?"

He swore at that, a profanity so explosively ob-scene that she cringed. "Save it, Olivia! I didn't come here to be raked over the coals yet again for some-thing over which I had absolutely no control!"

She shrugged contemptuously. "So, leave! I don't see anyone keeping you here against your will."

"Not until I've said my piece, which is simply this: it seems that you've carved quite a niche for yourself in hospital affairs, which means we're bound to cross paths frequently in the next month or two. I suggest that, unless you want to set every tongue in town wagging, you learn to leave your personal antipathies at home, because the job site is no place to air them and I won't put up with being made to look like a fool in front of my colleagues. Your little performance this morning will not be repeated, Olivia. Do I make myself clear?"

"Don't you condescend to me, Grant Madison! I'm no longer the insecure little twit you once knew. I haven't just grown older, I've grown up, as well. Meet the new me: Olivia Whitfield, B.Comm., fully accredited fundraising executive. It takes determination and guts to go out into the big world of business and hustle for bucks. But you wouldn't know about anything like that, would you, locked away in your pure, anti-bacterial ivory tower?"

"Holy cow!" he murmured. "I'm impressed!"

But he didn't sound impressed; he sounded highly amused.

"Listen to me," she hissed. "I won't put up with being treated like some feather-brained socialite playing at being important for want of something better to do! So the next time you get the urge to tell me to consult an expert, remember that I *am* the expert when it comes to finding ways for Springdale General to operate in the black, and if you *really* want to see that new equipment in CCU, you'd be well advised to put a lid on your ego and listen to me on the best way to go about getting it."

She hadn't rehearsed the tirade, but it rolled off her

tongue as smoothly and with as much fire as if she'd been practicing for weeks. She was breathless when she finished: breathless and triumphant. In the old days, she'd never have put him in his place so effectively that he was rendered momentarily speechless.

"Well," he said, when he finally found his voice again. "Well, well, well! Daddy's little girl seems to have grown up after all, and about time, too. Tell me, sweet face, how did you manage to slide out from under that big, controlling thumb of his?"

"After surviving ten months of marriage to you, it was a breeze, I can assure you!"

"Oh, come now, Olivia, I don't deserve that. They weren't all bad months. We had some memorable times."

"Too few to count, I'm afraid."

"Oh, really? Is that why you lost it on Saturday night? Because you couldn't remember how it used to be with us?" He shook his head. "If you're going to go over the top like that for no reason at all every time we happen to meet, you'll turn the next few weeks into one long soap opera for everyone else in town."

"I don't give a hoot what everyone else in town thinks."

Of course, it was a bald-faced lie, but, surprisingly, he bought it. Abandoning his contemplation of the flower pots, he strolled over to where she sat in the chaise with her knees drawn up to her chest so that he had no opportunity to subject her cleavage to further inspection. "You know," he said, looking down at her with a mixture of respect and regret, "if you'd shown half the backbone then that you've acquired since, we might still be married today."

"I don't think so. Say what you like about my father, but he was right when he warned me that you and I shared nothing in common. It's a miracle we stayed together as long as we did."

She ought to have known better than to bring her father into the discussion. The old light of battle sparked in Grant's eyes before her words had cooled on the evening air. "Nothing?" he echoed. "Oh, that's not quite true, Olivia. We shared something quite extraordinary—for a little while, at least."

"I suppose you're harping on sex again," she said, squirming a little under his gaze, "but I'm afraid it doesn't have any staying power when it's the only thing holding a relationship together."

"You're sure of that, are you?"

"Yes," she said, but he heard the betraying quaver in her voice and, like the predator he was, took immediate advantage of her weakness.

"Why don't we put your theory to the test, Olivia?" he murmured silkily, and before she could blink, let alone refuse him, he dropped down beside her on the chaise and kissed her.

How ridiculous that the same word used to describe a peck on the cheek should apply to the exchange which occurred between them at that moment. How preposterous that nothing Henry had been able to devise in the way of romantic overtures came even close to the utter seduction of Grant's mouth on hers.

He didn't touch her anywhere else. No hands sliding up her bare arms to find her throat and trace a daring line to where her bikini top clung tenuously to her breasts. No forcing her lips apart with his tongue to take possession of the dark and secret enclaves of her mouth. No doing any of those things she found herself wanting him to do. Just simple devastation with a touch as light as thistledown that lasted a second, and then two, and then three, and which left her aching in every pore. Hurting for something she had missed more than she'd ever dared admit.

The pain roared through her like fire, as though it had been lying in wait for the last eight years for just such an opportunity to destroy her. The starch went out of her spine, seeping away like water to expose the great arid desert where her heart had lain untouched for so long.

She felt the moan rise in her throat and did her best to smother it, but it escaped anyway, a pleading, shameless whimper of need. The fingers she'd knotted around her knees lost their strength and let her legs fall slackly apart, leaving her with nothing but the yellow triangle of her bikini bottom to protect her where she was, and always had been, so susceptible to his advances.

"Grant," she implored him faintly, begging him in that single word to tell her that he understood, that he felt the same, that he wanted her as rapaciously as she wanted him.

But, although she heard the unspoken words as clearly as if she'd screamed them from the rooftop, he either did not or he chose to ignore them. Or perhaps he listened instead to his own, more prudent inner voices, because, very slowly, he lifted his head and drew back from her and muttered, "I shouldn't have done that. It was a mistake. A very big mistake."

"Why did you do it, then?" she asked, tears trembling in her throat.

"To prove a point that no longer has any relevance

in either of our lives,'' he said soberly, and stood up. ''I thought it was important that we clear the air between us, but it would have been better if I'd found some other place to do it because I should never have come here, nor will I again.''

The sun still slanted across the garden, filming the surface of the pool with gold and leaving the air soporific with heat, but suddenly she was so cold that gooseflesh stippled her limbs and set her teeth to chattering. He would never know what a supreme effort it took for her to reply, ''So leave. Run off and play with your stethoscope. Learn to knit with it, for all I care. I'm sorry I don't have a butler to show you out, but I'm sure you'll find your own way.''

Just briefly, he paused, as though perhaps he had something more to convey, some small indication that he was not completely unmoved by what had happened between them. But then he straightened his shoulders and swung away.

Miserably, she watched as he strode across the patio, dwelling on the sight of him and trying not to remember the time when she'd had the right to explore all that height and breadth of sheer masculine beauty. When to hold him in her arms and welcome him into her body had been the joy of both their lives. When to reach up and kiss him for no reason other than that he was her husband and she loved him had been as natural and instinctive as breathing.

Gradually, his footsteps faded, and as the silence he left behind came pressing down on her so did the tears. Not because he had left her tonight, but because he had reminded her too vividly of the pain she'd experienced when he'd left her before. She had not known he could hurt her so badly a second time.

Since Henry was out of town on business, Olivia spent the following Saturday evening exchanging news with her friend, Bethany, who'd just returned from three weeks of shepherding her grade twelve art class through the galleries of northern Italy. But everyone else worth knowing attended the bi-monthly dinner-dance at the Country Club, and, by Monday, the town was buzzing with the news that handsome Grant Madison had squired Joanne Bowles to the affair and danced with her well into the small hours. Mrs. Bowles was reputed to be over the moon, according to the waitress at The Hanging Garden Café, where Olivia met Bethany for lunch that afternoon.

"Why do you care?" Bethany inquired, after the waitress had adjusted the angle of the umbrella over their table and left them to enjoy their meal in peace.

"I don't," Olivia said.

"I see. Then it must be the avocado shrimp that has you looking so green about the gills."

Olivia looked down at her salad and almost gagged at the glutinous concoction staring back at her. "I just never imagined Grant with another woman, I guess."

"Why on earth not, Olivia? Eligible men under fifty and over six feet are in short supply around here, or haven't you noticed? Add a full head of hair and all his own teeth to the mix and you've got a product calculated to have every woman under eighty drooling into her morning oatmeal."

"You're right, of course. When he puts his mind to it, Grant can be charming."

"Having only ever seen the man in photographs, I'm not in a position to say, but you obviously found him irresistible at one time. The adoration on your face in those wedding pictures you keep stashed at the back of your bedroom closet is pretty hard to miss.''

"I'd only just turned twenty at the time, and was easily dazzled.''

"And it takes more than great biceps, fabulous pecs and a good-looking face to impress you now, does it?''

Olivia thought of Henry, sweet, faithful Henry whose fair skin burned to a crisp in the sun and whose hair was thinning noticeably on top, but who would cut off his right arm before he'd hurt her feelings or make her cry. "Definitely!''

"Hmm.'' Bethany stirred her iced tea thoughtfully. "Then why haven't you trashed that wedding album? Why hang on to something you no longer value?''

"I don't know,'' she said. "I tried a dozen times to throw the damned thing away but I could never bring myself to go through with it. Once, I got as far as dumping the whole works in the garbage can, but the next morning I brought it back in again, cleaned it off, and put it back in its tissue-lined box.''

"Where neither dust nor grime nor light of day can damage its embossed white leather covers and the flawless memories they contain.'' Bethany looked at her meditatively. "Is that why you waited so long to divorce him, Olivia? Because you were still in love with him and hoping he'd come back to you?''

"Certainly not! What an absurd idea!''

"Well, you don't have to bite my head off. It's a reasonable enough question, given that you hung on almost two years before taking the final step to end things.''

Olivia grimaced apologetically. "You're right, of course, and I suppose the reason is that he was my first love and I had a hard time admitting that anything ugly could ever touch something so entirely magical and magnificent. I guess, in a way, that I still believed in fairy tales.''

"I didn't know he was your first love. I always assumed there'd been others before him. You were nineteen when you met him, after all.''

"Oh, I'd dated other men, but I was really just a girl playing at romance with a succession of suitors properly impressed by my father's position in the community and his wealth.''

But Grant, as she remembered all too well, had cared nothing about those, and in fact had despised her father—a mutual dislike which had flourished despite her efforts to effect some sort of truce between them.

"What's so special about money and power," Grant had scoffed, shortly after she'd started going out with him, "if a man's lacking in integrity?''

She'd been shocked. Nobody ever criticized Sam Whitfield, at least not in front of his daughter. "Are you saying my father's dishonest?'' she'd asked.

"Not in so many words, Olivia. But he's pretty big on self-interest.''

"What makes you think that?''

"Well, look at the way he controls you, for a start. You practically have to ask his permission to leave the house because he expects you to be there whenever he needs a maid or secretary or hostess.''

"It's only been that way since Mother died.''

"And how long ago was that?''

"Four years.''

"Plenty of time for him to hire someone else to pick up the slack, I'd say. Except it's more convenient this way because, unlike paid help, you can't—or won't—walk out when he goes too far. He's a bully, Olivia, and you're making a big mistake in letting him get away with it.''

''I don't mind,'' she'd said, half-scandalized at the idea of defying her father, and half-thrilled by the prospect. ''It gives me something to do, besides my volunteer work at the hospital.''

Grant had snorted in disgust. ''You need to cut those apron strings before they strangle you, sweet face, and put a little distance between you and your old man. You need to get a life—set that mind of yours to better use.''

''Hey!'' Bethany tapped her arm. ''Where have you gone, girlfriend? I feel as if I'm having lunch with a shadow.''

''I was just marveling at how sheltered and naive I was when I met Grant. I remember him telling me to grow up and make something of myself, instead of letting my father control everything I did.''

''Sounds like pretty good advice, if you ask me,'' Bethany said judiciously. ''Your dad does like to run roughshod over anyone who gets in his way, you know.''

''The trouble was, I was besotted enough to believe that marrying Grant was the answer, and immature enough to think that, as my husband, he'd run interference for me with my father.''

''I gather he didn't see that as part of his husbandly job description?''

''No. And if I'd been able to see past the… um…the sex—''

''It's okay to say the word out loud, Olivia. No one's going to brand you a hussy. Sex between a man and a woman is considered quite normal—and even preferable to some of the kinky things going on behind closed doors these days. So, to get back to what you were saying, if you'd been able to see past the sex, what then?''

''I'd have listened to my father, because for once he was right. He warned me that I was making the biggest mistake of my life, that nothing good would come of the marriage and that I'd live to regret it. But what woman pays attention to that sort of advice when she's in love and consumed with desire for a man?''

''Not you, obviously.'' Bethany grinned. ''Nor should you have. It's not up to the parents to choose their children's spouses, at least not in our culture. What did old Sam have against Grant, anyway? I mean, I could understand if you'd hooked yourself up with some shiftless bum who couldn't hold down a decent job. But we're talking Doctor's Wife, here, Olivia. Not too shabby a situation to find yourself in, by most people's standards.''

''But there were red flags going up all over the place, if only I'd had eyes to see them. Instead, I married Grant in a flurry of confetti, champagne and fantasies so fragile they never had a hope of surviving beyond the honeymoon phase. It took only a few months for me to wake up to the fact that real life wasn't going to live up to my girlish expectations and by then the damage was done. Too many things had happened.''

Bethany tipped her head to one side inquisitively. ''What kind of things?''

''Oh, just…things,'' Olivia said, trying to shrug the question aside.

But Bethany was having none of it. "Oh, come on, Olivia! We're supposed to be friends, and friends don't shut each other out like this. You seem to forget that I didn't set foot in Springdale until four years ago, and that the only Olivia Whitfield I've ever known is the super-confident, super-effective fund-raising exec who manages to coax money out of thin air to keep every charity in town afloat, particularly the hospital. She's not the type to run away from a challenge, so how come she didn't fight for her marriage?"

"Because, for all that he was a dedicated and skilled doctor, his treatment of me was cavalier, to say the least. For instance, you don't know the number of times, both before and after our marriage, that I'd spend an evening waiting for him to phone or show up as promised, only to be stood up in favor of more urgent hospital concerns."

"No, I don't know," Bethany said evenly. "But I do know that's what being a doctor's wife is all about. It strikes me you should have expected it *and* accepted it."

"That's because you're pushing thirty. But at barely twenty, and admittedly a bit spoiled, I wasn't prepared to take second place to a career whose demands never stopped. The way I saw it, if Grant had loved me as I loved him, he'd have put me first."

"Maybe, at that stage of his career, he didn't feel he had that choice."

"All medical interns are overworked, Bethany, but most still manage to find time to play, to nurture relationships, to commit to something other than medicine."

"And you didn't realize he was different from the rest before you said 'I do'?"

"Yes. But another flaw in my twenty-year-old's thinking was the belief that, once we were married, I'd be able to change him. He'd always had something of the gypsy in his soul, but I really thought that if I made home the most irresistible place in the world, he wouldn't be able to wait to come back to me at the end of the day."

"But people don't change, do they?"

"No. He didn't, and neither did I. He continued to be obsessed with his work and I continued to behave like a child deprived of her favorite toy. Worse, I became jealous of the people who saw more of my husband than I did—especially the women who'd also chosen to make a career in medicine. Why would he want to rush home to someone who had only her high school diploma to hang on the wall?"

"Because presumably he didn't fall in love with your high school diploma, you idiot. He fell in love with you."

"Not far enough," Olivia said bitterly. "If he had, he'd never have left me the way he did, especially not then."

"I'd ask what that means, except I don't think I'm going to get an answer, at least not right now." Bethany straightened in her chair and squinted at some point beyond Olivia's left shoulder. "Don't look now, but if your ex looks anything like his photograph, he just came out to the patio and is being shown to a table. And he has Joanne Bowles with him."

"Oh, good grief!" The small amount of salad she'd

managed to consume shot to the pit of Olivia's stomach like a bullet.

"You want to leave?"

"And have it seem that I'm running away? Not on your life! Let him leave, if he doesn't like the company!"

"Well, I don't exactly think he's seen you yet," Bethany said. "Right now, he's concentrating on Joanne, who's pulling out all the stops to keep his attention focused on her—and succeeding pretty well, I might add. If her neckline were much lower, we'd all be able to see what she ate for breakfast."

Over the sudden, crushing ache in her heart, Olivia said, "I don't care. I really don't. He can have lunch with whomever he pleases. It makes not a scrap of difference to me."

"So you say, Olivia, but it seems to me that you remember an awful lot about him—all kinds of details that most other women would have forgotten if, as you claim, they were over a man. Are you sure you're not still carrying a torch for him?"

"Quite sure. I have no feelings for him, one way or the other. In fact, he could come and sit at the same table with us and it wouldn't bother me."

"Oh, goody," Bethany said, with wry humor. "Because he's finally noticed you and he's on his way over. Plaster a smile on your face, kiddo, and try not to look as if you've just been dug up. All eyes in the joint are watching the latest episode in your personal soap opera."

CHAPTER FOUR

IT WAS just as well Bethany was there. She picked up the slack every time Olivia found herself at a loss for words, which was more or less the entire time Grant spent with them—except when the wrong words spilled out of her mouth, as if she had no control over either her tongue or her brain.

"Nice to see you again, Olivia," he said, looking at her expectantly.

She swallowed, staring mutely into her iced tea because he looked too handsomely distinguished to be believed, and frantically trying to think of a reply which wouldn't sound hopelessly trite or pathetically eager.

When the silence threatened to become awkward, he took a stab at ending it. "I hoped I'd run into you at the hospital over the last day or two so that we could get together for coffee and try to smooth over the way we left things the last time we talked."

"Um," she squawked, struggling to work the syllable past the desert her throat had become. "Ugh..."

Baffled, he turned to Bethany for help. She responded by raising her shoulders in a tiny shrug, as though to say, *Don't look at me. I no more know what's choking her than you do,* and volunteered, "She was busy working on the new seniors' housing complex. They're hoping to raise twenty thousand toward their on-site recreation hall."

"Very commendable, I'm sure," he said. "By the way, I'm Grant Madison."

"So I gathered. Delighted to meet you at last," she cooed, basting him in the warmth of her smile. "I'm Bethany Gilmore."

"You work with Olivia?"

"Uh-uh." Her blue eyes sparkled up at him. "We're just friends. I teach at Springdale High."

"A tough profession to be in, these days," he said, in his most deeply sincere and sympathetic doctor's voice.

That, and the way he looked Bethany over, as if she were a particularly succulent appetizer, set Olivia's teeth on edge. He'd always had a talent for making a woman feel she was the only creature on God's earth that mattered—at least until something more interesting cropped up. At nineteen, and relatively inexperienced, she'd swallowed such a bill of goods wholesale, but she'd have thought that, at thirty, her worldly friend Bethany would know better.

Instead, Bethany bloomed like a flower opening before the sun. "Not really, at least not for me. I teach art, which most kids enjoy."

Suddenly finding her voice, Olivia barked, "If the two of you are going to exchange life histories, why don't you take my seat, Grant, and I'll go and keep your date company? I don't imagine she cares for the way she's been dumped with nothing but a menu to keep her entertained."

She sounded like an embittered drudge who'd been robbed of her last dime, but she couldn't help herself. Once started, the venom just kept spewing out. Ignoring Bethany's start of surprise and Grant's theatrically raised eyebrows, she went on, "Or isn't one woman enough for you anymore, and you'd like all three of us hanging on your every word?''

''I was merely being civil, Olivia,'' he replied, the steely undertone in his voice matched by the icy blue glint in his eyes. ''You ought to try it some time. Most people your age mastered it years ago, to the enormous benefit both of themselves and those around them.''

''Well, you asked for that,'' Bethany said, staring after him as he made his way back to his own table. ''Good grief, Olivia, I've never known you to be so bitchy or rude. What came over you?''

Appalled, Olivia leaned her elbow on the table and covered her eyes with her hand. ''I don't have the first idea!''

''I think you do,'' Bethany said sagely. ''In fact, I think we both do. You're not over him, not by a long chalk. There's no other reasonable explanation. And I'm not convinced he's over you, either.''

''That's absurd! He couldn't wait to get away from me.''

''Can you blame him? The man practically did handsprings trying to be charming, but you acted as if he weren't even on the same planet.''

''Well, you certainly made up for it!''

Bethany's giggle rang out so infectiously that half the other patrons in the restaurant looked over to see what the joke was all about. ''Olivia, you can't possibly be jealous!''

''No.'' She grimaced, self-deprecatingly. ''That's one weakness I hope I have outgrown. It's just that all it takes is a certain look or word from him to make me feel as inadequate and pathetic as I was the day he married me. Somehow, no matter what I achieve, it's never quite enough for him to take me seriously.''

"If you want my opinion," Bethany said, "I think he'd be willing to take you very seriously, given half a chance.''

"He's already dating Joanne Bowles. That's hardly the behavior of a man pining for another woman.''

"It's hardly a declaration of marriage, either. You're seeing Henry. Should I take that to mean you'll be headed down the aisle before the summer's out?''

If that had ever been a possibility, Olivia thought with a sinking feeling, it was by no means a probability. Because everything had changed with Grant's return. She was no longer sure where she was headed. Or with whom.

He didn't expect to hear from her again. He didn't think he wanted to. Yet when the phone rang in his office the next afternoon, and he heard her voice on the other end, he couldn't repress a sudden surge of... What? Hope? Relief? Elation?

"Look, Grant," she said, getting straight to the point, "I'm calling to apologize for the way I acted yesterday. I don't know what came over me and I'm very embarrassed by the things I said. They were completely uncalled for.''

"Apology accepted," he murmured, chagrined to find his hand sweating on the receiver, even though the air-conditioner kept the room at a comfortable temperature.

"You were quite right when you said we both needed to get past our differences.''

Actually, that hadn't been quite what he'd said, but

now didn't seem like the time to quibble over minor details. "I'm glad you agree."

A pause shimmied down the line, fraught with undetermined tension, as if she was waiting for him to add something more. But for the life of him he couldn't imagine what.

Finally, she said, "Well, I guess that's all. I just wanted to set the record straight to avoid any further misunderstanding or awkwardness. You know how it can be when people run into each other unexpectedly."

"Perhaps we could eliminate that possibility by planning a specific meeting," he suggested. "That way, neither of us will be caught by surprise and we'll be less likely to say or do anything we might later regret."

"I'm not sure I know what you mean."

"We could get together for dinner."

"Dinner?" she repeated, as if he'd proposed something unspeakably crude.

"Why not? People have been known to do that, Olivia, for no other reason than that they're friends."

"Friends..." She rolled the word around in her mouth, as if she were trying to decide whether or not she could tolerate its flavor. "Well, I suppose it couldn't hurt. But I'd rather make it lunch."

"So would I," he said, lying through his teeth. Lunch would mean a quick sandwich in the hospital cafeteria, and he'd had something more leisurely and intimate in mind. "Unfortunately, my schedule's pretty full for the next three weeks. But we can make it an early dinner, if that'll ease your suspicions any."

"I'm not suspicious," she said, suddenly sounding as breathless as if she'd run a marathon. "I just never pictured you and me having dinner together again, that's all.''

Neither had he until a couple of minutes ago, but he wondered now why he hadn't thought of it sooner—for all the reasons he'd just stated, of course. "How about Thursday?" he said, riffling through the pages of his appointment calendar. "I'll be through here at the hospital by five and could pick you up between six and half past."

"Well, all right."

Hearing the doubt already creeping into her voice, he hastened to reassure her. "And, as I said, we'll make it an early night, since we've both got to get up and go to work the next morning. Nothing fancy, just a quick bite somewhere."

He hung up quickly, before she changed her mind. Then, leaning back in his chair, he propped his feet on his desk, clasped his hands behind his head, and contemplated the ceiling.

A month ago, if anyone had asked him why he'd leapt at the chance to spend the summer in Springdale, he'd have said to broaden his experience, to prove he could rise to the challenge of a senior position, and perhaps, in a very minor way, to rub Sam Whitfield's nose in the fact that the man he'd once scorned as not good enough to wipe the mud from his daughter's shoes had amounted to something. Yet from the elation he was currently experiencing, he'd almost think he'd come back with the express intention of making another play for Olivia.

Just as well that wasn't really the case. Because there wasn't a hope in hell they could ever make a go of things, not after the fall-out from their marriage the first time around. And he'd be willing to bet it wouldn't take more than one dinner to illustrate the point.

She dressed down for the occasion, just to prove to herself that this wasn't a date in the normal sense of the word. A full-skirted cotton dress with a hem that came mid-way down her bare calves, rope-soled wedgies, no jewelry but a simple gold chain around her neck and small gold studs in her ears, and no accessories but a clutch purse and a wrap in case the evening turned cool.

She thought, after a spritz of perfume and a final skim of lip gloss, that she was ready. Prepared to face her inner dragons. Able to remain sufficiently in control of herself that she could, as the saying went, walk and chew gum at the same time without too much trouble—or, in this case, sit across a table from him and manage to hold a rational conversation without accidentally sticking her fork in her ear.

Yet when the doorbell rang, ten minutes earlier than she was expecting it, and as she hurried downstairs to answer, the cartwheels in her stomach colliding with the lurching of her heart, she knew the only person she was fooling was herself. No amount of groundwork could prepare her for facing an evening alone with Grant Madison.

But her attack of nerves was premature. It was her father, not Grant, who stood on the doorstep. ''Ah, good, you're home!'' he said. ''When I saw him at the bank earlier, Henry mentioned you weren't seeing him tonight so I expected you'd be at loose ends.''

Uninvited, he stepped past her into the house, made his way to the tiny butler's pantry where she kept her liquor, and proceeded to pour himself a healthy shot of Scotch.

"Actually," Olivia said, following him, "I'm going out shortly."

"Well, it'll have to wait, because I want to talk to you about the new Pediatric Wing. We're way over budget and we're going to have to figure out ways to raise extra funds if we're to have it open on schedule."

"I already wrote up a proposal on that and sent you a copy, Dad, and I don't have time now to—"

"Well, make the time, damn it! This is important. And quit pacing about like that! Anyone would think the house was about to catch fire. Speaking of which..." he pulled a linen handkerchief from the breast pocket of his jacket and swabbed it around the back of his neck "...this heat is enough to kill a man. How are you enjoying the pool, by the way? Still think I went overboard with your birthday gift last year?"

"I've certainly appreciated it the last couple of weeks."

"Well, there you are, then." Wheezing slightly, he hauled himself up onto one of two stools at the breakfast bar and swallowed a mouthful of Scotch. "I still know best when it comes to what makes my girl happy. Now, about that proposal..."

It was Sam's usual mode of operation when anyone threatened resistance to his plans: a blunt reminder of past generosity, a finely timed pause to let the message sink home, then full steam ahead with his original agenda. He'd never change, Olivia thought wryly, but she, thank God, had!

"We aren't going to have this discussion right

now, Dad,'' she said firmly, ''because, as I've just mentioned, I'm going out. What I will do, though, is give you a copy of my original notes so that you can study them at your leisure. You can finish your drink while I look through my files, but then you're out of here.''

It took her a few minutes to locate the pages she wanted, then run off a spare copy—a few minutes too long, as it turned out. When she came back downstairs, Grant had arrived, Sam had discovered him, and the two were going at it with a vengeance.

''...no business just walking in as if you owned the place!'' she heard her father declare furiously.

''Cool your jets, Sam. Olivia's expecting me.''

''Not tonight, she's not. She's going out.''

''That's right, she is. With me.''

''Hogwash!'' her father roared. ''She wouldn't be seen dead with you!''

Taking the last four stairs as fast as her wedgies would allow, Olivia raced to put a stop to the fracas before it grew seriously out of hand. ''Cut that out this minute, both of you!'' she ordered, skidding to a halt in the kitchen doorway. ''You should be ashamed, grown men behaving like children! The pair of you can probably be heard clear across town.''

''Hey,'' Grant said, raising both palms in the air and backing away. ''Tell it to your old man. I'm not the one who started slinging insults. And tell him to knock off the booze while you're at it. He looks about ready to pop a blood vessel.''

''Dad?'' Suddenly anxious, she swung her attention to her father. He sat slumped against the breakfast bar, his breathing ragged and his color too high. ''Are you okay? Do you need your medication?''

"I will," he panted, "if I have to listen to much more of his bull. What's he doing here, Olivia? Tell me he's lying about going out with you tonight. Tell me you're not falling for his phoney charm a second time."

"Of course I'm not. We're having dinner together, that's all." She passed him the sheaf of notes. "Here, take these and look them over. If there's anything that's not clear or that you want to discuss, leave a message and I'll give you a call when I get home."

"I planned an early night, Olivia," he said, looking for all the world like a wily basset hound. "I've been burning the midnight oil too much lately and it's beginning to take its toll on my strength."

"I don't plan to be late," she promised, steering him to the front door.

Grant was standing at the back door when she returned to the kitchen. "Well," he said, staring out at the garden, "I see nothing much has changed, after all, despite your little spiel on independence the other night. You might have moved out of the main house, but when Sam says, 'Jump!' you still say, 'How high?'"

"He's an old man, Grant," she said wearily. "And even you can see that he's not well. Just because I'm in my own place and leading my own life doesn't mean I've forgotten he's my father. It doesn't cost me much to show him a little consideration."

"He doesn't seem inclined to return the favor. Or is it just when I'm around that he acts like a dog afraid of losing his favorite bone?"

"He's my father," she said again. "He worries about me. He doesn't want to see me get hurt."

"And having dinner with me is likely to cause you unmitigated pain, is that it?"

"Well, indigestion, certainly, if you plan to carry on like this all night. Perhaps we should cancel and get together some other time when you're feeling less cantankerous."

He swung to face her at that, the stubborn cast to his mouth reminding her of times past when he'd dug his heels in about something. "Not on your life, Olivia! I'm not letting that opinionated old goat dictate what I do or when, so grab your stuff and let's get out of here before he comes up with some other way to derail our plans."

They exchanged scarcely a word on the drive across town. He slouched behind the steering wheel of his car, a low-slung, racing green import with tan leather upholstery, which was every bit as luxurious as Ingrid from the deli had reported it to be, and glowered at the road ahead as if he had a personal score to settle with it.

She'd have liked to ask exactly where he was taking her, but, after one quick glance at his stony profile and his lean, strong hand wrapped around the gear shift as if he wished it were her father's throat, Olivia looked out of the window. The passing scenery was less disturbing.

Once across the river, he swung sharply left on the bluff and turned up the winding driveway to The Ambassador, Springdale's grandest hotel. Leaving the car with the parking valet, he ushered her through the lobby to the Riverside Room.

"I thought we were going to settle for something simple," she said, after they'd been shown to a window table overlooking the waterfall. "This place hardly fits the description."

"They'll serve you a hot dog, if that's what you want," he replied moodily. "Personally, I'm ready for something I can really sink my teeth into."

"Like my father, perhaps?"

He looked up from the wine list in time to catch her amused glance, and a grudging smile touched his mouth. "Am I being a jerk?"

"Yes," she said. "But I'm used to it, remember?"

He shook his head, self-exasperation written all over his face. "Is this how it was when we were married, Olivia? With him and me going at it tooth and nail all the time, and you getting caught in the middle?"

"The pair of you didn't often agree on anything, I must admit."

"And we still don't. By unspoken agreement, we keep out of each other's way at the hospital. I guess he feels he can let me run my own show since I'm not going to be here all that long. But I know he resents my having come back here."

His observation prompted her to ask, "Why did you come back, Grant?"

He didn't look at her when he answered, "You know why. Justin asked me to stand in as his locum."

"Justin could have asked any number of people. Why you?"

"He knew I was between appointments and could spare the time."

"You mean, the stint up north is over?"

"Heck, yes," he said, slapping the wine list closed. "It lasted less than three years. A man can take only so much of having his butt frozen ten months of the year and chewed raw by black flies the rest of the time. I moved out west to California, where the winters are tolerable.''

And now he was back east again. The more things changed, the more they stayed the same. "So you're still a gypsy," she said evenly. "The open road still lures you."

"And you're still a home-town girl. Don't you ever get tired of the same old faces and places, Liv?"

He'd been the only person ever to call her Liv, and then only when they'd been especially close. Hearing it now evoked such potent memories of the good times they'd shared that her breath snagged painfully in her chest. "As a matter of fact, I left town shortly after you did. The following September I moved to Windsor, and spent the next four years working on my degree."

"No kidding! That must have shaken things up some on the home front."

"Some," she admitted, not about to tell him that she hadn't been able to face Springdale without him. There'd been too many places they'd gone together, too many people who knew them as a couple. She hadn't known how to bridge the enormous gap he'd left in her life.

He watched her for a moment, drumming his fingers on the table the whole time, then gestured at the menu she held. "Decided what you're going to have?"

"No," she said, disappearing behind the leather-bound cover before he noticed the sheen of tears in her eyes. They'd started their marriage with such high hopes, could have had so much, and ultimately had settled for so little. In retrospect, the waste of it all struck her as unforgivable on both their parts. They'd had no right to squander such a rare and wonderful opportunity.

"You want a drink before we order?" he asked,

"No," she said again. She was already ridiculously weepy, without adding alcohol to the mix.

"Wine with dinner, then?"

"I don't think so. Some sparkling water would be nice, though."

"Oh, give me a break, Olivia! A glass of wine isn't going to compromise your integrity. Your morals will remain intact, I assure you. How about a nice Chardonnay? You used to love that."

I used to love you, she thought miserably. *Please don't keep reminding me of that.*

For a little while, he seemed to read her mind. After a brief toast to friendship, he steered the conversation into safely neutral channels. They talked about the new reservoir up in the hills behind town, the restoration of the courthouse square in the center of town, the fabulous view from the window. He told her about a hiking trip he'd taken in the Andes. In return, she told him about her vacation in Greece, and relaxed enough that she almost began to enjoy the evening.

That changed, though, after their salad had been cleared away and they'd been served their entrées. Just as she was about to take a bite of her grilled sea bass, he suddenly asked, "Does he make you happy, Olivia?"

Mystified, she put down her fork and looked at him. "Does who make me happy?"

"Henry."

"Oh," she said, taken aback as much by the intensity in his tone as the question itself. "Yes, I suppose so."

"How?"

"How?" She shrugged. "I'm not sure, exactly."

"Well," he said, studying his wine as if he expected to find fruit flies swimming in it, "if what you say is true, it's not because he's the most fantastic lover in the world."

"He's very kind, Grant," she said, not about to be drawn into another discussion of Henry's sexual prowess or lack thereof. "Very considerate. Furthermore, we share the same interests. When we do things together, I don't feel as if he's wishing he were with someone more exciting. He's a very... steady sort of person."

"Have you ever had a falling out?"

She blinked in surprise. "Now that you mention it, no. Never."

"Are you going to marry him?"

"He's yet to propose."

"That's not what I asked. We both know he'd jump at the chance to put a ring on your finger. The question is, would you let him?"

"Why do you care?"

"I want you to be happy, Olivia. I always have. And, let's face it, he's the kind of man your father would welcome as a son-in-law. You wouldn't get any flak from that quarter if you marry Henry."

"My father doesn't choose my husbands, Grant," she said, remembering what Bethany had said.

"He certainly didn't the last time around, or you and I never would have made it as far as the altar."

"There was nothing personal about his objections.

He thought I was too young to marry anyone, that's all.''

"Garbage! He thought you could do better."

"He never said that," she protested, but there was no conviction in her voice because he'd hit the nail right on the head. Right up to the morning of her wedding day, her father had done everything he could to get her to call the whole affair off. Threats, pleas, emotional blackmail, bribery, he'd tried them all, along with a litany of Grant's faults that would have filled a book. "He—"

But Grant saw the flush stealing over her face, and stopped her before she dug herself in any deeper. "I was there, Olivia, remember? Everyone else in that mausoleum of a church might have had their eyes on you, but I was watching him. He'd have had me lynched, if he could."

"Well, I was watching you," she retorted, the memory as clear as if it had happened only yesterday. "You're very quick to point accusing fingers at my father for his past sins, real or imaginary, but you weren't exactly blameless yourself, Grant. From the look on your face when I came down the aisle, you might have been about to spend the rest of your life on death row. It's a miracle I didn't find myself left at the altar, because you were about ready to bolt."

"Yes, I was," he said, with devastating candor. "But the point is that I didn't."

"Only because things had gone too far for you to back out!"

"Oh, come off it, Olivia! Do you honestly believe I'd have let a five-tier wedding cake and a few hundred overdressed guests coerce me into doing something I didn't really want? I was in love with you, for crying out loud!''

"You cured yourself of that pretty quickly though, didn't you? Being stuck with what you so derisively used to refer to as your 'child bride' soon lost its appeal.''

"Because the child refused to grow up.''

"I was barely twenty years old, for heaven's sake!''

"And acting as if you were still twelve, turning to Daddy every time the big, bad husband didn't toe the line! He did his damnedest to ruin our marriage and you made the job a whole lot easier. When it came down to a choice between him and me, you chose him. The worst mistake I ever made was agreeing to live under his roof.''

"It was your decision to take him up on the offer so that we wouldn't have to worry about paying rent until you'd finished your internship,'' she snapped, pushing aside her half-finished meal.

"If I'd known what it was going to cost in terms of our marriage, I'd have told him to shove his charity! No man should have to compete with his father-in-law for his wife's loyalty and affection. Bear that in mind before you jump into marriage with Hank from the Bank. You might be able to lead him around by the nose now, but that could change if, every time he wants to make love to you, he has to worry about Sam walking in and catching him in the act.''

"My father *never* did that to you!''

"Not for want of trying! He'd have liked nothing better than to find me with my pants down around my ankles and fill my bare butt with buckshot!''

"Hush up!" she whispered, scandalized. "That's no way to talk in a public place."

He crowed with laughter at the fire scorching her cheeks. "You've turned into a prude while I've been gone, Olivia! We used to do a lot more than just talk. I remember a few times when we actually *did* it in public—and without benefit of matrimony, too. Hank doesn't know what a treat he's missing!"

"You're such a pig, Grant Madison!"

"Yeah," he agreed, with a shameless grin. "Ain't I just!"

"There's not a chance we could ever be friends."

"No," he agreed, the grin still firmly in place. "Not a snowball's chance in hell!"

She tossed down her napkin and reached for her purse. "I should have known an evening with you would turn into a fiasco! Thanks for the dinner and I'll find my own way home."

"We're being watched, Olivia," he said calmly, lifting his glass in a mocking toast. "So unless you want all the local hens cackling about you over their morning coffee tomorrow, sit down and stop making a scene."

Even before he'd finished speaking, she could practically feel inquisitive eyes boring into the back of her neck. A moment later, a shadow fell across the table, and Muriel Bowles, decked out in black lace and emeralds, trilled fruitily, "Dr. Madison, what a surprise, running into you here! And with your ex-wife of all people—how are you, Olivia, my dear? You haven't forgotten my little soirée tomorrow night, have you, Doctor? Joanne is *so* looking forward to seeing you. Again."

"I haven't forgotten," Grant said, the very picture

of gallantry as he rose to take Muriel's well-preserved hand.

She preened and flung Olivia a triumphant little smile. "I'd ask you to come, too, dear, but I'm sure you and Henry have other plans."

Olivia opened her mouth to decline graciously, but some perverse demon sprang to life inside and answered for her. "Actually, we don't, and we'd love to come."

"Well, my goodness!" Muriel Bowles murmured. "How very...nice."

"Walked right into that one, didn't you?" Grant sniggered, as the woman stalked away. "Tell me, sweet face, what excuse are you going to give for changing your mind at the last minute?"

"I'm not," the demon piped up. "Henry and I will be there. With bells on."

CHAPTER FIVE

IN FACT, Olivia wore her mother's antique pearls around her throat and at her ears, and the pearl ring set with diamonds which her father had given her when she turned eighteen. And a silk designer creation in gorgeous rose-pink, with strappy sandals to match. She had her hair done, and her nails, and just for good measure threw in a facial, too, emerging three hours later from the best salon in town looking as chic as a French model.

Appearances, she determined, splurging on her favorite perfume just as Henry drove up to her front door, might merely be skin-deep, but they went a long way toward bolstering a woman's confidence. And hers had dwindled to near extinction since her rash acceptance of Mrs. Bowles' reluctant invitation.

As things turned out, however, she could have shown up in prison drab for all the good it did her. From the moment she arrived at the Bowles' ostentatiously handsome residence, the evening slid steadily downhill. Despite at least sixty guests milling about the terrace and manicured lawns, plus an army of waiters hired for the occasion, her gaze dissected the crowd and immediately homed in on Grant—or, more accurately, Grant and his companion.

All teeth, cleavage and couturier white chiffon, Joanne Bowles was the very picture of a smugly complacent huntress, clinging so tenaciously to her quarry that they might as well have been joined at the hip.

Henry surveyed the scene with almost equal satisfaction. "Shall we mingle, Pussycat? I see one or two clients with whom I'd like to have a little informal chat."

"Go ahead," Olivia said, accepting a champagne cocktail from one of the waiters and pretending to admire the ice sculptures dominating the center of the buffet table. "I'm happy to people-watch for a while."

"You'll be okay on your own?"

"Of course I will, Henry!" she said, rather more sharply than he deserved. But it was difficult to remain unruffled, with Grant making a spectacle of himself not twenty feet away and half the town there to witness it. For heaven's sake, couldn't he see how pathetic he looked, lapping up his new girlfriend's avaricious attention? Joanne was ogling him as if he were edible and she hadn't eaten in a month!

At the other end of the table, Ingrid from the deli arranged a parsley wreath around a tray of hot canapés. "I never took you to be the kind who liked rubbing salt in her own wounds, Olivia," she observed, in a voice that could be heard a mile away. "Here, hon, help yourself to a stuffed mushroom quick. It'll give you something else to do besides foam at the mouth while you watch another woman trying to steal away your man."

"He's not mine and I certainly wasn't watching him. And even if I were, what good would it do me? The only thing he's got eyes for is that dress his date is almost wearing." Then, despising her shrewish tone almost as much as the bitchiness which had inspired it, she added, "Not that I can really blame him. It is rather lovely."

Ingrid snorted disparagingly. "Personally, I find roadkill more attractive. If that young woman were any skinnier, she'd have to stand twice to cast a shadow."

Determined to dredge up a little charity, no matter what it cost her, Olivia said, "Well, perhaps it's her sparkling company that has him so engrossed."

"Joanne Bowles has all the personality of a cucumber, Olivia, and well you know it. If you weren't so full of stiff-necked pride, you'd do him the favor of wrestling him away from her before she smothers him."

To her horror, Olivia found the idea all too appealing. Quickly, before temptation got the better of her, she popped another canapé in her mouth and strolled to the edge of the terrace. Immediately below, an ornate stone fountain comprising gargoyles and nymphs sent jets of water cascading into a huge scallop-shaped bowl. It provided a much less disturbing show than the one taking place behind her.

It was also quite noisy, which probably explained how, shortly after, Grant managed to sneak up undetected and murmur in her ear, "Since you didn't seem inclined to come and say hello, I thought I would."

His elbow was so nearly touching hers on the balustrade that she could feel his body heat. His aftershave wafted faintly on the air. If she'd turned her head, she'd have been within kissing distance of his mouth. She knew because, although she refused to look him in the eye, she could smell the pleasant blend of toothpaste and coffee on his breath. "You're on call tonight, aren't you?" she said.

"Yeah. How'd you guess?"

"Because you never touch alcohol if there's a chance you might have to work."

"True." She felt rather than saw the speculative gaze he turned on her. "I'm flattered and surprised that you remember."

Oh, she remembered—far too much! She remembered the nights after they were married, when he'd be kept working late at the hospital and she'd fall asleep with only his pillow for company. And how often, in the small hours, she'd come awake to find his hand sliding down her belly and between her thighs, or his mouth at her breast, or even the silken heat of him buried deep inside her and the first tremors of pleasure already washing over her.

She remembered, too, those times when he hadn't come home at all, sometimes not for three or four days at a stretch. But then, suddenly, the door would open and he'd be there, his jaw shadowed with beard, his eyes ringed with exhaustion.

On those occasions, she'd be the one to waken him. She'd take his hand and lead him into the huge bathroom adjoining their bedroom. He'd follow, docile as a sleepwalker, so wilted with fatigue that he could barely raise the energy to peel off his hospital greens.

She'd turn on the twin shower heads, adjust the setting so that the hot water came pulsing down like a thousand reviving fingers to massage the weary muscles in his neck and shoulders, and, stripping naked herself, would follow him into the glass-walled enclosure.

"Sorry, sweetheart," he'd mutter, practically asleep on his feet. "The spirit might be willing but the flesh isn't up for anything much just now."

"Hush," she'd say, soaping away the antiseptic

odor clinging to him. "It's enough that you've come home."

She remembered the feel of him beneath her hands, the smoothly muscled strength of him, the texture of his skin, his hair, the abrasion of his beard against her fingertips. She remembered his eyes falling closed, his lashes plastered into drenched black spikes against his cheeks, and how he'd be swaying on his feet so that his body brushed against hers.

Sometimes, for all that he'd thought it wasn't so, his flesh would prove itself more than willing, and he'd reach for her then. She'd wind her arms around his neck and her legs around his waist. Bracing himself against the shower wall, he'd cup her bottom in his hands and slide so deeply into her that there hadn't been a part of her he hadn't seemed to touch. Their mating would be fast and furious, culminating for him in a climax whose intensity drained away all the stress of work and left him relaxed enough that he'd sink fathoms deep in sleep for hours.

They'd been the good times, the times when there had been no anger, no resentment, no insecurity. The times worth remembering. And they sprang to life in her mind so vividly that it came as a shock to hear him say now, "We've been apart a long time, and I'd have thought, from the way you acted when you got here tonight, that you'd have buried all memory of our marriage."

"I have," she said, thoroughly ticked off to find herself aching with regret for the mistakes she'd made and wishing she could put things right again. How *dared* he have such an effect on her! "And, frankly, you were so busy cosying up to Joanne, I'm surprised you even noticed me at all."

Whatever else his shortcomings, Grant was no fool. He picked up on her blunder at once. "If I didn't know better, Olivia, I'd think you're jealous. But that wouldn't make sense, would it? According to you, not only were we a romantic disaster, we can't even be friends, so why would you care who you catch me with?"

"I don't," she said. "But that's not to say that I—"

"You've made a big enough point of telling me you've moved on with your life, after all, and you surely know I've done the same. Or did you think there weren't any women up north and that all I'd have to keep me warm on those long winter nights were thoughts of you?"

"Of course I didn't think that!"

But the sick sensation churning inside put the lie to her claim. The absurd fact was, she'd chosen to believe he'd left her because there was no room in his life for anything other than medicine.

Their dreams had not coincided. She'd wanted a house on a tree-lined street with a park on the corner; a future built around children, and a husband who'd put his family first and be there on birthdays and holidays. He'd aspired to loftier ambitions, to taking his expertise north of the Arctic Circle, to areas so remote that people still died needlessly for want of proper medical care.

Whenever she'd tried to picture him—and it had been often, particularly during the first three years after their separation—she'd always seen him braving a blizzard to save a life or perhaps bring a new one into the world. She'd imagined him climbing aboard a helicopter to reach some far-flung settlement, performing delicate surgery with only the most basic equipment on hand. Being a hero, god-like in his selfless dedication.

But not once had she imagined him finding comfort in some other woman's arms. That he had, left her eyes scalding with sudden tears.

She tried to snatch back her control before misguided grief undid her. But the lump in her throat continued to grow, and when she attempted to swallow it away, a pitiful little half-sob formed in its place.

''Are you crying, Liv?'' Grant inquired, astonished.

''Yes,'' she said, swiping at her blurred vision, since there was no point in denying the obvious.

''What for?''

''Because seeing you and listening to you reminds me how it feels to be rejected. Damn you, I thought I'd found happiness again, but now I wonder if I'll ever trust myself to really love another man.'' Her voice was rising, drowning out the splash and gurgle of the fountain, but there was little she could do to stop it. It was as if a floodgate had suddenly opened inside. All the emotion she'd somehow contained after he'd abandoned her gushed out in one long, impassioned torrent. ''Why did you have to come back, Grant? All you've done is resurrect a lot of painful ghosts. Why couldn't you just have stayed away? What made you—?''

''Hey,'' he said, closing his hand over her arm. ''Remember Justin's wedding? Get a grip, sweet face, unless you want to be the star attraction again here, tonight. How much have you had to drink, anyway?''

''Not nearly enough,'' she cried. ''I've never needed help in making a fool of myself where you're concerned. But if I'm embarrassing you in front of your new girlfriend, by all means feel free to go running back to her side.''

''And leave you alone to face this crowd of vultures?'' He flung a scornful glance at the well-bred crowd, the closest of whom were watching them with covert attention. ''Fat chance!''

Using his body as a shield, he hustled her down the steps and across the lawn to the topiary garden on the far side of the lily pond. ''Here,'' he said, piloting her along the gravel paths to a bench tucked away in a sort of hedged alcove whose entrance was carved to resemble a large keyhole. ''This is a bit more private. Have a seat and collect yourself.''

He thrust a clean linen handkerchief into her hand and crouched in front of her while she mopped at her ruined make-up. She sniffled and blew her nose and tried to hide her face, because she knew how she must look with heaven only knew how much mascara streaking her cheeks. But he was having none of that.

''Okay,'' he said, forcing her chin up so that she had no choice but to meet his gaze. ''Are you going to tell me what this is really all about? And don't say it's Joanne Bowles, because you and I both know she's not my type. And I doubt old Hank's yours if running into me again can unravel you like this.''

''I don't know what it's all about,'' she wailed, trying once again to cover her face with her hands as a fresh spate of tears threatened.

He sighed and, sitting down beside her, drew her head against his chest and said resignedly, ''Yes, you do. We both do. And I guess we've reached the point where it's not doing either of us any good to go on pretending otherwise.''

She had no idea what he meant. Furthermore, she didn't care. It was enough that she could hear his heart beating beneath her ear, and that he held her in his arms again. She had not felt so complete for over eight years and it was worth any amount of future misery just to be held by him like this again.

"It's us, Liv," he went on, resting his chin against her carefully arranged hairdo. "You and I. Apart, we can make a good enough show of moving on with our separate lives that we fool everyone, including ourselves, into believing what we had is over. But put us in the same town, where we keep running into each other, and the whole charade falls apart."

Too surprised by his words to remember that she didn't want him seeing her cry, she planted her hand flat against his shirt-front and pushed herself upright to stare him full in the face. "What are you talking about? Just the other night, you agreed we can't even be friends."

"Because being friends isn't enough. We've always wanted more from each other. Maybe we wanted too much. And maybe…" His chest rose beneath her hand in another massive sigh. "Maybe it would have been better to let sleeping dogs lie."

"What's that supposed to mean?" she cried. "I'm confused enough as it is, without your talking in riddles."

"Exactly. The day Justin Greer got married, you were the most together woman on the planet. Then you saw me and the cracks started showing. Look at you now, Liv. You're a mess, and, frankly, so am I. When I agreed to fill in for Justin, I told myself I was just doing an old friend a favor and that I'd have done the same if he lived in the middle of Africa. If I'd had the slightest inkling I'd find myself caught up in us again, I'd have turned him down.''

"But you knew I still lived here?"

"Yes. Justin did happen to mention that small item of news.''

"Then you must also have known we were bound to run into each other, sooner or later.''

"Hell, Liv, I was counting on it! But I thought enough time had passed that we'd both be able to handle it. I'll even admit to a certain curiosity about you, but if you'd asked me a month ago what made Justin's offer so attractive, I'd have said it was to flaunt the fact that I've risen from the rank of lowly intern to fully qualified cardiologist and don't need your father or his favors to garner respect among my colleagues.''

"You never did, Grant," she said. "Whatever else my father thought of you, he always respected your medical skills.''

"Grudgingly, at best. In his view, the only people who should aspire to professional status are those born with money and social standing. Blue-collar kids like me, from working-class neighborhoods, never quite measure up, no matter how hard they try. We might know how to wield a scalpel, but we'll never learn how to use a dinner knife and fork.''

He was thirty-five years old, intelligent, talented, sophisticated, and able to charm apples off trees when he put his mind to it. But just then she saw in his blue eyes the ghost of the defiant boy he'd once been. *If it hadn't been for my mother going out to work, we'd have been on welfare,* he'd confided to her, soon after they'd started dating. *My dad was a shiftless bum, and had nothing but scorn for what he referred to as my lah-di-dah ambitions to better myself. But I showed him!*

"Don't you know you don't have to prove anything to anyone anymore?" she said softly, reaching up to touch his jaw. "Can't you see you've come far enough that what my father thinks doesn't count?"

"Your father isn't the problem now, Olivia, and if I'm honest, I know he wasn't then. We were. If we'd believed in each other, and in our marriage, nothing he or anyone else could have done would have driven us apart. How the hell did we manage to screw things up so badly?"

"I've been wondering the same thing myself," she said.

His gaze scoured her face, dwelling on each feature in turn, beginning with her mouth and ending at her eyes. "Has too much happened to make it worth a second try, sweet face?"

Had it? Could they ever forget the hurt or get past the resentment? Was wanting something enough to make it happen, or were there some things that couldn't be mended, regardless of how hard they tried? "I'm not sure, Grant."

He cupped her chin in his hands. "No guts, no glory, Liv. Wasn't that our motto, once upon a time?"

"But what if we can't make it work? I don't know if I'm brave enough to risk failing again."

"What if we go about things differently? Take our time, say, and talk honestly about the things that went wrong before and figure out if we can live with the kind of changes we'd have to accept to make a go of things this time?" He smiled and stroked her cheek with a tenderness he'd never shown during their marriage, when devouring passion had ruled the day.

"What if we agree to put sex on the back-burner and concentrate instead on establishing a more solid foundation for our relationship? Would that persuade you to take a chance?"

Oh, she wanted to! And the relief of finally daring to admit it without guilt or reservation left her giddy. Still, caution warned her against allowing euphoria to blind her to reality. "We had some pretty serious disagreements, Grant. The way you reacted to my pregnancy—"

Abruptly, he removed his hand and sprang to his feet. "Yes," he said, pacing the small enclosure as if it were a cage offering no escape. "I know. And although it comes too late to make any difference, I'm sorry. My only excuse is that, at the time, I felt you got pregnant on purpose—a last-ditch attempt to bring me into line and save a marriage which had been circling the drain practically from the word go. It wasn't that I couldn't mourn that baby's loss, Olivia. I had my moments of regret and grief, too, and they weren't easy to deal with. But I also knew we weren't in any shape to take on parenthood, so, yes, the miscarriage was a blessing, as well. We were screwed up enough. We had no right to drag an innocent child into the mix."

He came to a stop in front of her and, reaching down, pulled her to her feet. "There's no point in even thinking about a reconciliation if we can't put all that behind us. Can you do it, Liv?" he asked, looping his arms around her shoulders. "Or is the miscarriage always going to come between us?"

He towered over her, his face shadowed by approaching dusk, his touch warm and comforting. Beyond the hedge, the faint strains of music and laughter drifted on the still air, but the party could have been happening on another planet for all that it touched them in that quiet corner. No sex, he'd said, but its potent magic swirled between them, silent as sea fog and just as potentially dangerous.

"I hope we can," she said, disengaging herself from his grasp. "But now's not the time to try to find out. Henry must be wondering where I've got to."

"Screw Henry," he said hoarsely, sliding his hands down her back and splaying his fingers over the swell of her hips. "Henry doesn't figure in any of this."

"That doesn't give me the right to just disappear on him without so much as—"

He silenced her as only he could, at once and completely, by closing his lips over hers and stifling the words in a kiss that rocked her soul. She felt her resolve melting, slipping away like water between her fingers. "Liv…" he whispered against her mouth, the urgent thrust of his hips confirming the hunger threading his words. "Sweetheart…"

Self-recrimination could come later—and it would, with scorching condemnation—but the fleeting perfection of the here and now was too tempting to resist. She softened in his embrace, savoring the moment.

"Grant?" Another voice, a woman's raised in inquiry, floated over the hedge and footsteps crunched on the gravel path leading to the alcove. "Are you in there?"

He inhaled so sharply the air whistled through his lips. *"Damn!"*

Unsteadily, he thrust Olivia away and skimmed his hand through his hair. She tugged at her dress as guiltily as if he'd half stripped her, and, spinning away from him, put a respectable six feet of distance between them just in time. A second later, a swirl of white chiffon obscured the keyhole entrance and there was Joanne, with Henry in tow.

"We thought we saw the two of you disappear in this direction," she said, her gaze darting suspiciously from Grant's granite expression to Olivia's flaming cheeks. "I've been looking everywhere for you, Grant."

He stared her down without blinking. "Now that you've found me, what can I do for you?"

She pressed her lips together in undisguised annoyance. "You could remember this evening's being held in your honor and make yourself available to other people besides your ex-wife," she pouted.

"Olivia and I wanted a few moments of privacy to catch up on each other's news."

"I see." And she did—far more than she should have. Her glance raked over Olivia with a thoroughness that would have made a worm squirm. "In light of the trouble my mother's gone to to make this evening special, is it unreasonable of me to ask that you choose another time and place to do that?"

"No, it's not," Olivia said. "I do apologize for monopolizing you like this, Grant, and Joanne's quite right. You really ought to be circulating."

He opened his mouth as though to object, but then seemed to think better of it and said instead, "I guess we've said everything that needs to be said, so why don't we all get back to the party?"

But Olivia hung back. "First, I'd like to have a word alone with you, Henry."

He didn't seem surprised, and waited patiently until they were alone, then said, "You really don't need to say anything, Olivia. I know I'm not the most imaginative or exciting man in the world, but I hope I'm sensitive enough to recognize when the woman I'm with is in love with someone else.''

His quiet dignity completely undid her. ''I'm sorry, Henry,'' she whispered brokenly.

''Why? You didn't plan this. It just happened. Or perhaps it's more that it never stopped. I won't say it doesn't hurt, because it does. I'd hoped that, in time, you'd be able to forget Dr. Madison and find something in me that you could come to care for, but I guess it just wasn't in the cards.''

''I wish it were,'' she said. ''I'm truly fond of you, Henry, and I know that, with you, I'd have been safe.''

''Loving and being in love aren't about safety, Pussycat. They're about passion, and that's something you and I have never shared. Perhaps if Grant hadn't come back we could have found a kind of placid happiness together, but I think we both know it would have been a second-best choice, especially for you.''

''I'd have been willing to give it my best shot,'' she said, swamped in remorse. She and Henry *could* have had a good life, if only she'd never known Grant.

''It isn't how much you can bring to a relationship that counts,'' he said, ''it's how much you withhold. You'll give everything to Grant Madison, and if it's not enough, you'll find a way to give more. I can't fight that, Olivia, and I won't demean myself by begging. But I want you to know that if you ever need a friend, I'm here.'' He straightened his shoulders, tugged his tie in place, and offered her his arm. ''Now, shall we join the others?''

''No,'' she said, her voice full of tears. ''I've had

enough for one night. Will you take me home, Henry, please?''

''Of course,'' he said. ''I'm willing to do whatever it takes to make you happy.''

His words echoed over and over in her mind after he'd dropped her off at her front door and she'd changed out of her dress into a cotton robe and gone out to sit by the moonlit pool. Was she mad to choose Grant's maybe-promises over Henry's solid commitment? Hadn't she learned that excitement wasn't enough to steer a marriage away from the rocks, that it took more than sex and fascination to create lasting contentment? Had she learned *nothing* from her past mistakes?

''Dear Lord,'' she whispered, touching her forehead to her bent knees, ''what have I done?''

CHAPTER SIX

HER father asked pretty much the same thing when he heard, though with somewhat less restraint.

"Have you lost your mind?" he bellowed, catching her in the hospital parking lot the following Thursday afternoon. "You've got the nerve to stand there and tell me you've thrown over a decent, respectable man like Henry Colton for a drifter who's already proved he cares only about himself? How many times are you going to let Grant Madison leave the imprint of his shoe all over your back before you come to your senses, girl?"

"Calm down, Father," she said, wincing as the bellow escalated to a full-throated roar. He'd been out of town at a golf tournament for the last four days, and, given that all their professional lives were so closely intertwined with Springdale General, she'd known there was slim chance he could be kept in the dark for very long, but she hadn't counted on the gossip reaching his ears quite so soon. "I don't know where you got your information, but you've obviously—"

"Where do you think I got it?" he boomed, thumping the roof of her car with his fist. "The whole damn hospital's enjoying a feeding frenzy over the fact that you're spending every spare minute with the man. Coffee on the roof garden, lunch in the cafeteria, cosy little walks together around the grounds—my God, the only thing I haven't heard is that you're sleeping with him again!''

''Not that it's anyone else's business, Father, but I'm not. Nor are we planning a second race to the altar. We're merely…exploring possibilities. As for Henry, he and I have talked the whole thing out and arrived at an understanding.''

''Understanding, my eye! I saw him this morning, Olivia, and he looks like hell. And if you persist with this ridiculous…*experiment*, I'm telling you now that it'll put me in my grave.''

''Typical,'' Grant said, when she reported the meeting to him that evening. Because of conflicting schedules, they'd had no chance to get together earlier in the day, so they'd arranged to meet for a quick dinner at one of the river-front cafés. He'd known the minute she arrived that she was upset. ''Sam pulled every stunt in the book to try to break us up before, and succeeded pretty well, so you can bet your last dollar he'll try the same thing again now. The question is, are you going to let him?''

''No. Those days are long over. But he does have a bad heart, and when he gets himself in the kind of state he was in today, it scares me.''

''He's counting on that, sweet face. He's very good at blackmail.''

''I suppose you're right.'' She poked at the lime twist in her water glass and sighed. ''I think what really set him off was that we're being so public about seeing each other.''

''For the very good reason that we both decided it wasn't a smart idea to spend too much time alone if we want to keep things…'' he rocked the spread fingers of his right hand back and forth "...on an even keel from the sexual standpoint."

"I know."

"It's the sensible route to take."

"I know," she said again.

But knowing and accepting were two different things, and "sensible" was no match for the driving hunger which possessed her every time they were together.

To be so close that she could touch him—to know how it felt to be kissed and held and possessed by him, and not be able to respond to those urges—distorted the parameters of their relationship as much as their rushing blindly into another sexual liaison would have done.

"We did make this decision together, Liv," he reminded her, watching her closely.

"Uh-huh." She looked down and concentrated on smoothing the napkin lying across her lap in an effort to wrestle her runaway hormones under control.

"So why the incipient tears?"

She swallowed and blinked. "You're too observant."

"It goes with the medical territory, sweet face, and you forget that I know you very well. Are you so upset by your dad that you're having second thoughts about us?"

"No," she said, absolutely certain on that point, at least. Anything with him was better than nothing without him, and only when she'd dared face that truth had she realized the emotional wasteland she'd been living in since their separation. "I'm just not finding this platonic angle as easy to deal with as I thought it would be, that's all."

"And you think I am?" He pulled his chair closer and took her hands in his. "You think I'm enjoying not being able to make love to you? Do you know how many cold showers I've taken in the last week? How often I've been tempted to change the rules and just carry you off to some quiet inn for the weekend?"

"Would it be such a mistake to do that, Grant?" Even a stranger couldn't have missed the naked pleading in her voice, but she didn't care. "I'm sorry if that makes me sound spineless and overeager, but the time for subterfuge ended the night we pledged to try to resurrect our relationship."

"Not 'relationship', Olivia," he said. "What we're trying to revive is the love. But we both know it's much too early in the game to consider whether or not we're going to succeed, and the fact that you can't even bring yourself to say the word should tell you that you're not ready for the intimacy that goes with it. So, yes, it would be a mistake, and I'm not prepared to jeopardize how far we've come just for the sake of getting you between the sheets again.

"On the other hand..." He grinned, that devilish, disarming grin she'd never been able to resist. "I'm not made of stone, and when you make suggestions like that and turn those big beautiful eyes my way, a certain part of my anatomy leaps to attention and is hard to ignore. So cease and desist, woman, unless you want to be publicly embarrassed again."

"Oh, Grant, honestly!" She dissolved, the tears streaming down her face this time induced by helpless laughter. "You know just how to make me feel better!"

"They do say laughter makes the best medicine,

ma'am.'' But his attempt to look suitably sober fell pitifully short of the mark. ''Finish up your pasta salad and let's blow this joint. The doctor prescribes a refreshing walk along the river before he sends you home.''

''You could come back to my place for a nightcap, instead,'' she said. ''If we make it short and sit at opposite ends of the patio, we should be able to stay out of trouble.''

''Not a good idea, sweetheart. The kind of trouble you invite is too tough to resist. In any case, I've got a consultation this evening that couldn't be rescheduled.''

He didn't like lying to her, not even indirectly. But the time had come to have things out with Sam Whitfield and make sure he understood the ground rules. Because no way was that bastard going to louse things up a second time.

He waited until after dark before making his move. Rather than risk having her see him as he drove past her front door, he left his car parked on the road outside the estate and took a side footpath that came out near the old stables. He remembered the way very well from the times in the early days when he'd come sneaking in to meet her after her old man thought she was safely tucked up in bed.

Whitfield House, a grand old colonial built around the turn of the century by her great-grandfather, stood quiet in the night, its windows staring blankly out on the moonlit lawns, the Virginia creeper covering its walls turned inky black by the shadows. The place might have been empty for all the signs of life it showed, but when he rang the bell, a light appeared beyond the stained glass panels set in the wall on either side of the entrance. A minute later, the imported English butler who'd served the family for years opened the front door and did a double take when he saw who was standing there.

"Evening, Edward," Grant said affably. "Is His Lordship at home?"

"I don't believe he's expecting visitors, sir."

"He's getting one anyway. Tell him I'll make it short, but I'm not leaving until I speak to him."

"One moment, sir." Leaving the door respectfully ajar, Edward disappeared.

A short while later, Sam showed up in carpet slippers and a maroon brocade dressing gown, a cigar clamped between his teeth. "What the hell do you want?"

"Good evening to you, too, Sam. And, thanks, I'd love to come in."

"Get off my property before I have you arrested, Grant Madison," the old curmudgeon threatened, and tried to shove the door closed in his face.

But Grant was prepared. Bracing one hand against the solid oak plank, he said, "Not until you and I arrive at an understanding, Sam. So where's it going to be? Out here, where Edward can listen in to every word, or some place more private?"

Eyeball to eyeball, they glared at each other, but as Mexican stand-offs went, this was no contest. Grant wasn't about to give an inch and Sam knew it. "You've got five minutes," he allowed, tramping down the main hall to a wing at the back of the house. "We'll talk in here."

"Here" was the library-cum-den, where, from all appearances, he spent most of his time. A television was tuned to a news station. A book and about a week's worth of newspapers were scattered on the carpet beside a leather wing-back chair next to the fireplace, and a tray holding a brandy decanter and an almost empty glass stood on a small occasional table close by.

"Well? Get on with it, man!" he snapped, topping up his drink and not bothering to offer one to Grant. "I don't have all night."

"Then I'll come straight to the point. Olivia and I are starting over, and I don't want you or anyone else messing with that. You did more than your share of interfering the first time around but I won't stand for it again. She'll always be your daughter, Sam, but she's no longer your little girl. She's a grown woman with a mind of her own. So back off and let her lead her life the way she sees fit."

"And if I don't?" He tried the eyeball act again, but the uncertainty in his gaze robbed it of effect.

"Then I'll fight you and I'll win," Grant said.

"You seem to forget who you're taking on, Madison. I carry a lot of weight in these parts. One word from me and you'll find yourself bounced out of town so fast it'll make your head spin."

Grant laughed. "You still put your pants on one leg at a time just like the rest of us, old man, and, short of catching me in gross professional misconduct or a felony, there's not a thing you can do to get rid of me before I'm ready to leave. And when I am, I'll take Olivia with me."

"And you call yourself a doctor!" the old fraud lamented, pressing a veined hand to his chest and staggering to his chair. "Even a layman could see I'm not a well man, yet you come in here, full of bluster and threats, and expect my blessing when you're doing your best to kill me.''

"You're as tough as nails and we both know it. But so am I, Sam, *so am I*! More to the point, I make Olivia happy, and if you care for her half as much as you claim to, that should count for something.''

"And how long is it going to last this time, Madison? Until your next harebrained scheme to eliminate disease from some godforsaken place no normal person would want to live in? Until she doesn't jump on your command? Until there's another baby in the offing that you're not ready to accept responsibility for?''

"I made my share of mistakes in the past," Grant admitted grimly. "I've also learned from them.''

"And she paid for them! You talk about making her happy, but her chances of that were a hell of a lot better when Henry Colton was the man in her life. Why in the name of heaven did you have to come back and spoil things?''

"If she was all that happy with him, why weren't they married? Why was she so ready to turn to me?''

"Because…because…!'' The steam filtered out of him like air escaping a balloon. Leaning back in the chair, he closed his eyes. "Damned if I know,'' he said dispiritedly.

"Maybe you should quit trying to figure it out and look after your own interests for a change. If you really want to stick around long enough for Olivia to make you a grandfather, you need to start taking better care of yourself.''

"You're a bit late with the medical concern, Doctor.'' He sighed and flung Grant a glance which, though loaded with resentment, nevertheless held a glimmering of respect. "But you're not afraid of a fight; I'll grant you that. You never were. And at least a man knows where he stands with you. All right, have it your way for now. But I'll be watching you. Put a foot wrong with my girl, and I'll be all over you like a dirty shirt. Meanwhile, since your five minutes is up, do me a favor and show yourself out."

It wasn't much of a victory, but it was more than he'd ever achieved before, and suddenly he wanted to share the flavor of it with Olivia. Whistling under his breath, Grant strode down the main driveway and stopped outside her front door. Over the chirp of tree frogs, the soft, rhythmic splash of water from the pool behind the gatehouse told him where he'd find her.

Stepping over a flowerbed, he followed a paved path around the side of the building and vaulted over a fence into the back garden. Except for the light in the pool itself, the area was in darkness, but he could see the pale shape of her towel flung across a chaise and there was no missing her.

Hair streaming out behind her, and as close to naked as he'd seen her in years, she completed lap after lap in a graceful crawl. Not until she started to haul herself out of the water did she realize she was being watched. She gave a startled gasp and with a soft scream dunked herself in the pool again so that only her head was visible.

"It's only me, Liv," he called out. "Sorry if I scared you."

"Scared me!" She reared up again, creating a little eddy of waves around her waist. In the strangely phosphorescent green half-light, she looked like some sort of dark-eyed water nymph. "You almost gave me a heart attack!"

"I seem to be having that effect on a lot of people tonight," he said, increasingly mesmerized by the sight of her as she hoisted herself up on the pool deck and tipped her head to one side to squeeze the water from her hair.

"Your consultation didn't go well?"

"Better than I expected, as a matter of fact." Deciding that the sooner she covered up all that lovely flesh, the better it would be for both of them, he picked up her towel and held it out like a nervous matador tempting a bull. Hah! Some bull! "I had a meeting with your father."

"Oh, Grant, you didn't!"

"I did," he said, shaking the towel a little.

Still, she kept her distance, seemingly unaware of the water reflecting shimmering lights over every sleek contour of her body. Shee-oot! "About me, I take it?"

"About us," he said. "Here, cover up. You'll get cold."

"It's still eighty degrees out here, Grant. Hardly what you'd call cold." Hooking a hand on one slim, bare hip, she continued to observe him from a distance. "I gather things didn't go well?"

"As a matter of fact, they did. Sort of," he said, going to her since she seemed disinclined to come to him, and wondering what mysterious force of nature was holding the flimsy bits of her bikini in place when, from all the anatomy he'd studied, they should be lying round her ankles. "Sam and I might never be friends, but I think we understand each other. Here, let me dry your hair."

He passed the towel around the back of her neck and mopped the dripping ends. She leaned into his touch, letting the weight of her head rest against his hands. "Why didn't you tell me you were going to see him? I'd have come with you."

"It was something to be sorted out between the two of us, man to man."

"Man to man!" she scoffed, laughing. "That expression died out years ago. Don't you know the politically correct term these days is person to person?"

Her whole body swayed toward him when she laughed. Close enough that the tips of her breasts brushed damply against his shirtfront. Too close. "I shouldn't have come here," he said hoarsely.

The glance she turned on him was as knowing and ancient as Eve's. "Why did you, then?" she said, winding her arms around his neck.

"Because," he croaked, "I'm a devil for punishment. Better back off, sweet face, unless…"

"Unless what?" She whispered the words into his mouth on a long, sweet exhalation.

"Look, Liv, we made an agreement."

"I know," she sighed.

But they could have signed it in blood for all the good it did him. Deliberately or otherwise, his tongue skimmed her lips and learned the truth about forbidden fruit being the sweetest. He tasted them again, more thoroughly, and felt his control slipping away as their soft, moist inner surface closed around his tongue. So like that other part of her, the part no other man but he would ever know.

The towel slid down past her shoulders. His hands followed, finding her waist, bare and cool in the too brief bikini. Her hips trembled against his, a minor earthquake of cosmic proportions. He thought he would burst.

Blindly, he inched his fingers inside the elastic of her bikini bottom and closed his hands over her slender buttocks, kneading their softness and craving to feel her fused just as tightly around him. It had been more than seven years since he'd last buried himself inside her, but the remembered ecstasy left him aching unbearably for an encore.

"Take off your clothes," she begged, her fingers urgent at his shirt, his belt, the zipper of his blue jeans. "Be *with* me, Grant."

"I am," he said, afraid his lungs were going to seize up on him. "More than you know."

"But all the way!"

She was killing him! Light and deft, her fingers wove their magical torment, snaking inside his shirt, down the front of his fly, etching the shape of him straining against the fabric. Hell and heaven weren't supposed to gang up on a man like this, disguising agony as delight!

He wondered if he could wait long enough to carry her upstairs to her bed before losing himself inside her, and decided not. Not when he could take her right there on the grass, the way he had the first time.

The first time…the wrong time….

"Honey," he muttered, crunching his eyes shut in misery and holding her away from him. "Sweetheart, forgive me."

"What for?" Her own need cried out in the question, raw and desperate. "Grant, please! We both want this."

"Oh, yes," he groaned, swiping at the sweat beading his forehead. "And it would be all too easy to give in to the wanting. And a whole lot smarter not to, because every time we ran into difficulties in the past, we turned to sex to find the solution. It became our panacea, the easy way to distract ourselves from getting to the root of our problems. I won't do that again, Olivia.''

Her mouth drooped with disappointment. Shivering despite the night's humid heat, she crossed her arms over her breasts and looked off to the side, at the petunias turned the color of vintage port in the dark, and the flowers on the jasmine vine gleaming like pale stars. ''I never thought I'd have to beg you to make love to me,'' she said bleakly. ''Before, no matter how bad things were, you were always willing.''

''But it wasn't enough, Liv,'' he said, wrapping the towel around her and able to pull her into his arms now that he'd wrestled himself under control. ''In the end, we needed more to keep our marriage afloat. Let's not make the same mistake again.''

She leaned her head on his shoulder and let out a long, quivering sigh that winnowed sweetly up the side of his neck. ''I know you're right. I just didn't know it was going to be this difficult.''

''It won't be forever, sweetheart,'' he said, and wondered when he'd become such a sucker for inane platitudes. He'd be telling her suffering was good for the soul next!

Giving a little shake, she stepped away from him. ''Okay, enough of feeling sorry for myself! How about some coffee?''

''I don't think so.'' He caught her chin between his thumb and forefinger and kissed her hard. ''We've pushed our luck far enough for one night. I'll call you tomorrow.''

He was over the fence when he thought he heard

her call out something. He couldn't be certain, but he thought she'd said, "I love you."

He hoped he was wrong. Like making love, it was too soon for that sort of declaration, but she'd always been too generous for her own good when it came to giving away her heart. She'd never learned that saying "I love you" wasn't enough by itself. It took trust as well, something which had been noticeably lacking the first time around.

Slow down, Olivia, he thought. *Don't make it any harder than it has to be for either of us. I don't want your broken heart on my conscience if things don't work out the way we hope.*

CHAPTER SEVEN

IT WAS as well the hospital's annual carnival and Sunflower Ball kept her occupied through early August, otherwise Olivia would have gone slightly mad. The new Grant, though delightful, appealing and altogether too exciting, dismayed her a little with his restraint. After that night by her pool, they spent very little time alone together, and she had to subsist on chance meetings, mostly at the hospital.

They'd run into each other at the elevator, or in the cafeteria line-up, and he'd smile at her over the heads of the people around them, the kind of smile lovers exchange. Warm, secretive, conspiratorial. And her chest would fill to bursting with love for him.

"Don't let me keep you," he'd tell her, far too often, in the days leading up to the ball. "I know you've got a full slate right now."

But I'd like you to keep me, she wanted to tell him. *I'm never too busy for you.* Only the memory of how firmly he'd declined her blatant invitation to make love before deterred her from begging again now. She still had some pride left.

But then she'd see him stop to speak to a patient, his face and manner full of sympathetic understanding, and she'd wonder how he could be so compassionate with a stranger's needs and fears, yet so indifferent to hers.

He waited until the week before the event to suggest they attend the ball together. "You left it so late,

103

I was beginning to wonder if you'd invited Joanne instead,'' she said, relief making her careless.

She recognized her mistake at once. The old wariness crept into his eyes and he took his time before replying, ''I sort of hoped we'd got past that kind of silliness, Olivia. If you don't know by now that Joanne's of no more interest to me than a fly on the wall, what's it going to take?''

''Nothing,'' she said contritely. ''I don't know why I even said such a thing. It's just that…oh, Grant, I want things to work out for us and time's slipping away much too fast. Justin will be back from his honeymoon in another three weeks and what then?''

''I've got a few ideas,'' he said mysteriously.

It was enough to keep her hopes alive, but barely.

Bethany came over and had dinner with her, three days before the big weekend. ''What are you wearing on Saturday night?'' she asked, as they lazed by the pool in the evening sun.

''I bought something new.''

''*New?* Good grief, Olivia, you've got enough formal gowns to outfit half the women in town! What did you need something new for?''

She'd wondered that more than once herself since her impetuous purchase the previous Monday. Too pricey and definitely elegant beyond anything anyone else would be wearing, the gown had nonetheless stopped her dead in the street when she'd caught sight of it draped sensuously over a gilt chair in the window of Monica's Boutique. Strapless, clinging, and shimmering with crystal beads, it was not designed for the flat-chested or the faint-hearted. ''Well, I am going with Grant,'' she said, as if that were any sort of explanation.

Apparently, it made perfect sense to Bethany, who gave a hoot of laughter. "Do I smell entrapment here, or what? Does the poor guy have any idea what you've got in store?"

"None at all," she said. "I intend to surprise him."

She succeeded, though not quite as favorably as she'd hoped.

"Holy cow!" he exclaimed in hushed awe, when he came to pick her up on Saturday evening. "That is some outfit, Olivia!"

"You like it?" Brimming with anticipation, she twirled around, the sheer silk cashmere scarf that went with the dress floating behind her like angel's wings.

He coughed. "I like it."

In her mind, she'd marked the coming evening as a sort of defining moment in their relationship. For four weeks they'd shared jokes and meals and opinions, exchanged gossip and dissected their shared past with a thoroughness that would have done a forensic psychologist proud. They had worked at becoming friends, at learning to trust one another, at getting to know what made the other tick. But the one thing which reigned uppermost in her mind—where they were really headed—remained in limbo.

It wasn't enough, at least not for her. Love and intimacy were an essential part of the mix if a man and a woman were to commit to each other in the fullest sense, and though she was long past the age where she pinned her expectations on *things*, she'd seen the dress as the talisman which would bring about the culmination of her dreams. For him to respond to it with such lukewarm enthusiasm sent an eddy of disappointment flooding through her.

"You like it?" she echoed. "That's all?"

"No." He backed away from her as if she were some kind of wild animal about to attack. "I kinda like you, too."

Like? she wanted to shriek. *Is that the best you can come up with? We've been liking each other for weeks! What will it take to bump things up a notch? Or is this as far as it goes?*

But that kind of emotional outburst had cost her dearly when she'd been married to him, so, schooling her features to reveal nothing of her frustration, she said, "How nice. Would you care for a drink?"

"No, thanks."

"Then we might as well leave."

"Might as well," he agreed.

From the way he behaved on the drive over to the Country Club, one could have been forgiven for thinking he'd had to be bribed into being her date. Beyond an occasional remark, he barely spoke, and once they arrived he could hardly wait to be rid of her.

"That woman who heads the social committee— Daphne What's-Her-Name—is making a beeline for you. I guess, with it being one of the biggest fundraising events of the year, she wants to make sure you've covered all the angles," he said, eyeing the cocktail lounge with undisguised longing, as if pickling himself in alcohol was the only way he'd make it through the evening. "I'll wait for you in the bar."

"I'd have thought you'd take more of a professional interest in how things are going, seeing that the money we raise tonight is being funneled directly to the cardiac unit. I recall a meeting where you made quite an impassioned plea for new equipment."

"I just happened to be the stand-in spokesman at

that meeting, Olivia,'' he replied, his raised eyebrows telling her he'd noted the vinegary tone in her voice. ''I'm not the head of CCU, nor am I going to be around long enough for any changes that might come into effect to impact any patients I'm currently treating. Tonight is a purely social occasion for me.''

''Well, heaven forbid I should bore you with shoptalk, then!'' As much as the narrow skirt of her dress would allow, she swept away. When he called out to her to stop being such a ninny, and started after her, she dodged around a clump of guests chatting in the lobby and disappeared into the ladies' room.

She knew she was overreacting, but, in the blink of an eye, time had seemed to switch into reverse, rolling back to when she'd been the clinging tagalong half of a marriage in which an up-and-coming young doctor bound for greater things hadn't needed the encumbrance of a wife given to sulking if he didn't shower her with his undivided attention whenever he was with her in public. Well, he might not recognize that things had changed since then, but she'd teach him differently before the night was out!

Seating herself on one of the velvet-covered stools before the vanity, she fished a lipstick out of her evening bag and, although it didn't need it, touched up her mouth. She helped herself to hand lotion. She tucked a wisp of hair into place. And when Daphne Jerome cornered her, she made no attempt to escape and listened with feigned delight while the woman rattled on about all the pots of money they were making.

She let Grant Madison stew in his own juice for a full twenty minutes! Then, poise restored, she sauntered into the cocktail lounge.

The crowd had thickened. Among the faces she recognized were her father and Henry, as well as Bethany and her fiancé, Matthew Black. Grant stood in a corner near the long windows overlooking the river valley, deep in conversation with a group of other doctors. He didn't even notice her return.

Nodding and smiling so determinedly her face ached, she accepted a glass of sherry and circulated on her own. "The dress is a knock-out, you look stunning, and there isn't a man in the room who wouldn't give his eyeteeth to have you hanging on his arm," Bethany said, when she stopped to chat with her. "So if you and Grant are serious about reconciling, how come you're avoiding each other? Did you have a fight?"

"Of course not," she said, too brightly.

"Then why don't you go over there and smile at him the way you're beaming at everyone else? He keeps casting glances your way."

Then let him be the one to come to her! She'd be damned if she'd grovel for his attention!

They didn't meet up until dinner was served nearly an hour later. "So, you having a good time?" he inquired, a conversational gambit which vied with chatting about the weather in terms of safe neutrality.

"Very," she said starchily. "And you?"

"Well, it's a change to be in the same room with your father without there being fireworks. He's been almost civil tonight. Wanted to know all about where I was going when I leave here. If I didn't know better, I'd think he was anxious to see the back of me."

His eyes were full of teasing laughter, but the reminder that he'd soon be leaving filled her with fresh dismay. Quickly, before the all-too familiar lump formed in her throat, she turned to the man seated on her other side. In his late forties, and married with five children, he posed no threat to her composure.

After dinner, Grant made the socially correct gesture and asked her to dance. They circled the floor like polite strangers, with him holding her a decorous foot away and both his hands where they belonged. She stared past his right shoulder with a fixed little smile on her face, and responded to his half-hearted attempts at conversation with the briefest answers she could manage. It came as a mutual relief when the music stopped and he could turn her over to some other, more willing partner.

He, meanwhile, did the rounds, sometimes sitting at other tables and chatting with several people, sometimes inviting a woman out on the floor. Once, he danced with Joanne Bowles, draped for the evening in exquisite turquoise lace. From the other side of the room, Olivia pretended not to notice and saw everything.

They made a striking couple, she had to admit. Joanne at five-ten plus heels came closer to his six-two than Olivia could ever hope to achieve. Her long legs moved in perfect sync with his, her eyes, though not quite on a level with his, coming close enough for her to gaze adoringly at him without tripping over her feet.

Olivia could hardly blame her. There wasn't a man in the room who came close to him for sheer masculine beauty. He might still prefer blue jeans in his off-hours, but when it came to dressing to the nines, he stood alongside the best of them in his faultlessly cut dinner suit.

Suddenly, he looked up and caught Olivia staring. He smiled a little and rolled his eyes as if to say, *Rescue me!* She offered a wintry smile in return and looked away.

How long things would have continued in that vein was anybody's guess, but as it drew close to eleven o'clock he decided he'd had enough. Drawing her determinedly onto the dance floor again, he said, "How long are we going to keep up this nonsense, Liv?"

"I don't know what you mean."

"Quit lying. You know damned well what I mean, but if you want me to spell it out for you, I will. You've been ticked off at me since I showed up on your doorstep tonight. I'm not sure why, but I can tell you I'm getting pretty tired of being given the cold shoulder. If I've done something wrong, either spit it out or get over it."

"All right," she said, her voice tight with anger. "I'll tell you why. I'm tired of being your best buddy. If all you want is someone to walk along the river with, go buy yourself a dog, preferably one that'll retrieve on command. If you want to discuss world politics, join a debating club. But if you want me, then start showing it. I bought this dress to impress you. I thought—I hoped it would make you sit up and take notice of the woman inside it. I was foolish enough to think it might…it might…"

She choked into silence before she disgraced herself completely and blinked furiously to keep her vision clear.

"Is that what this is all about?" he said, incredulously. "You really think I'm the only guy in the place not totally dazzled by the way you look? Good Lord, woman, you can't be that naive! You know the only reason I'm keeping a decent distance is that I don't trust myself up close with you. We've talked about this already a dozen times.''

''That's the whole problem,'' she quavered, losing her battle with the embarrassing tears. ''All we ever do is talk, usually in a roomful of people, and, while there might be safety in numbers, I'm getting tired of it. I need to feel close to you. Instead, I sense that you're pulling away, and I'm afraid I'm going to wake up one morning and find you gone. If that's what you really plan to do, please just tell me now, because I can't go on like this, waiting for the other shoe to drop.''

He reared back and stared at her in consternation, then pulled her against him, *really* against him, for the first time in weeks, and buried his face against her hair. ''Oh, sweetheart!'' he murmured. ''Honey, baby, please don't cry! I never meant to make you feel like this.''

But the dam had burst again, uncaring that neither the time nor the place was right, and, once started, there was no stopping it. It sometimes seemed to her that she'd done nothing but cry since the day he'd blown back into town.

Realizing the situation was beyond her, he took charge, waltzing her inconspicuously out of the ballroom and into the garden, then shepherding her around the outside of the clubhouse to the parking lot.

He bundled her into his car, and while everyone else continued to dance the night away he drove her home, holding her hand all the way and kissing the back of her fingers every once in a while.

Once inside her house, he stood before her and ran

his hands up and down her arms, his face a study in remorse and frustrated longing. "I promised myself I wouldn't let this happen," he said huskily. "I told myself we wouldn't let sex be the determining factor."

Afraid he was about to talk himself into another postponement of the inevitable, she stopped him. "Don't," she said, pressing her fingers to his mouth. "Please, no matter what tomorrow brings, don't pull away from me now. Don't analyze the whys and what-ifs. I'm asking for one night, Grant, not guarantees of happy ever after."

"That's good," he said, "because there aren't any, not in life and not in love."

Love: he'd said the word, and even though not in the context she'd have preferred, it was a step forward. "I know. But I also know that playing it safe all the time isn't what real living is about, and if I have to risk having my heart broken to find out if we have a future together, it's a chance I'm prepared to take."

"Even if your life is turned upside-down again?"

"I survived losing you once before, and if I have to, I'll survive it again. But right now I need you, Grant." She shrugged, and her voice was laden with tears again when she continued, "I never thought I'd have to beg you like this. I thought I had too much pride. But pride doesn't count for a damn thing where love's concerned. And whether or not you decide in the end that you want me won't change the fact that I do love you, with all my heart. Perhaps I always have and was just too young and foolish to know what I was throwing away when I initiated divorce proceedings."

He stopped her then, with the kind of kiss he hadn't allowed himself in weeks. She heard the groan that tore loose inside him, deep and dark and primitive, as all the safety barriers he'd erected for both their sakes came crashing down. She tasted the yearning he could no longer disguise.

Before she had time to savor the moment, he swung her off her feet and took the stairs two at a time to her bedroom. He lowered her to the side of the bed, held her face between his hands and toured her mouth with his in desperate anguish. "Okay, you win," he muttered, lifting his head at last and tearing off his tie as if he were strangling. "But I don't mind telling you, you scare the hell out of me!"

She smiled and closed her eyes and, leaning forward, pressed her lips to his throat. She felt the tremor that shook him, felt his fingers tugging the dress down her body an agonizing fraction at a time until her breasts lay bare before him. Although the midnight air brushed cool across her exposed flesh, his hands traced avenues of heat that warmed her soul and sent the blood rushing through her veins.

She wanted more of that heat, wanted to feel his nakedness imprinted against hers so that not an inch of him was kept from her. She wanted to taste him, to feel the forceful energy of him driving into her, again and again, until they were both consumed by it.

Feverishly, she attacked the gray pearl studs down the front of his shirt. They popped loose, flying in every direction. The matching cufflinks followed. The fabric of the shirt was damp from her tears but the skin beneath was warm and vital.

"I've always wanted you, Liv," he whispered, his

breath tortured, "but never more than this last month. It's been a living hell seeing you and not feeling I had the right to touch."

"You can touch me now," she said, trailing kisses over the planes of his chest and circling his navel with her tongue.

He did, in exquisite detail. He took the dress and stripped it away from her in one long, smooth sweep. Reverently, he removed her panties and the narrow garter belt which held up her sheer silk stockings. And she lay on the bed and she watched him, carving every second indelibly in her mind so that, if this should turn out to be but a moment in time never to be repeated, she'd be able to recall how, when she lay naked before him, he adored her. How he strung kisses from her breasts to her belly, how he touched her with his tongue and sent rapture shooting through her like a thousand silver arrows.

She wanted total recall of how he closed his eyes and mouthed her name silently as he hovered above her. How he shuddered as the climax he couldn't control took hold of him.

She wanted all this because she'd taken for granted, the last time they'd made love, that such intimacy would be theirs to enjoy for ever. She'd neglected to imprint it on her memory and had, instead, immersed herself completely in the pleasure only he could give. But in the lonely days after he'd left her, all she'd had to sustain her were fragments of remembered ecstasy, touched with starshine and moondust. She would not make the same mistake again.

Yet, try as she might, she could not retain her detachment. Her body responded to him just as it always had, with complete abandon. She clung to coherence, gasping at the vicious greed attacking it, and felt herself slipping away and drawn down into the dark and glorious vortex of fulfillment. Her last impression before she succumbed to the force of it was of the hot sweet proof of his passion spilling into her.

After, they lay side by side, awash in moonlight, and touched each other, full of wonder at the rediscovery. Stroked each other's faces and limbs. Kissed one another long and deeply. Simply looked at each other, as if they'd never get their fill of the sight of each other.

She served breakfast by the pool the next morning. He awoke to the smell of freshly ground coffee and found her in the kitchen, a short terry robe covering all that delicious flesh he'd found so irresistible the night before.

"Could you take a couple of weeks off from work?" he asked her, as they lingered over hot sweet rolls and fresh fruit.

"I suppose so, yes. My time's pretty well my own," she said. "Why, what do you have in mind?"

"I thought you might like to drive across country with me to Vancouver. We could do it in easy stages, stop a couple of days in the mountains, and just see how we get along, away from the goldfish bowl of Springdale."

Her face lit up. "Oh, Grant, it's a wonderful idea and I'd love to! What made you decide to ask me?" A becoming blush tinted her cheeks. "Was it last night?"

"Last night was the clincher, sweet face. The idea's been fermenting ever since we got together again and now seemed as good a time as any to mention it.''

"I've never been to Vancouver, but I'm told it's beautiful.''

"It's a great place to visit,'' he said, "but it's also very different from what you're used to, so I guess the big question is, could you ever see yourself living there in the event that we decided to take another run at marriage? And it strikes me that the only reasonable way to find out is for you to spend a bit of time getting the feel of the place.''

More starry-eyed than ever, she jumped up from her chair and hurled herself into his lap. "Marriage?'' she squealed, practically throttling him. "Grant, did I hear you right?''

Her shining excitement reminded him of a child on Christmas Eve, so full of wonder and trust that only good things would be waiting for her tomorrow. It worried him a little. So far, their relationship had posed no real threat to her established way of life, but what if she found she couldn't cut the apron strings which tied her to Springdale? Could he be the one to make the kind of concessions necessary for them to be together?

He thought about the staff position waiting for him at St. Paul's, one of the best teaching hospitals on the west coast. And about the penthouse apartment he'd leased overlooking English Bay and the park. Was he prepared to give it all up? More to the point, was he prepared to move back to Sam Whitfield's territory and all the attendant irritations that would entail?

"It's a bit premature to talk about marriage just yet, Olivia. Let's just take things one day at a time and see where it leads us. For all we know, you might be sick of the sight of me after a week of my undiluted company.''

She swung herself around so that she sat straddled on his lap and kissed him. Boy, she knew how to kiss! That mouth of hers should have been declared a restricted weapon! It drained him of every last atom of sense and left him writhing at the mercy of his hormones. And, from the sexy little smile creeping across her face, she was well aware of the fact.

''I've created a monster,'' he moaned.

''Oh, my,'' she said craftily, reaching down and running her fingers knowingly over him. ''And here I thought I was responsible for this.''

''Hussy,'' he said, parting the lapels of her robe and fondling the sweet curve of her breast. ''You don't have a stitch on under this thing.''

She flicked her tongue between his lips, a tempting thrust that left him aching for more complete union. ''I thought I'd save you a bit of time, Grant. You never know when you might get called in to the hospital,'' she purred, arching her spine sensuously and offering herself to him.

He felt her dampness on his thigh, saw her nipples darken into tight buds, heard her breathing shift gear as he ran his thumbnail down her sternum and over her belly to her pubic bone.

Well, hell, how could a man be expected to conjure up a little finesse in the face of such enticement? She had no time to do more than gasp with pleasure before he'd inched down his briefs and was inside her and homing in on the closest thing to heaven he'd ever known. She closed around him sleek as a glove, her narrow hips gyrating in blatant enjoyment.

''Hot damn!'' he whispered against her mouth,

dazed as the blood thundered through his veins. Morning sun, a summer breeze and Olivia convulsing in mindless abandon: this was the stuff dreams were made of!

Luckily, the drums of passion weren't beating so loudly that he didn't hear a car door slam and heavy footsteps plodding around the side of the house. How he got her off his lap without doing himself lasting injury was nothing short of miraculous; that he hadn't stripped off her robe a blessing. He just had time to yank his briefs into place before her father appeared at the edge of the patio.

"I thought that was your car out front," he said, his gaze missing nothing. "Did you stop by for breakfast?"

"No, Sam," he said, deciding he might as well brazen it out since he clearly was in no position to affect affronted dignity. "I've been here since last night."

For a second or two, Sam assumed his old pit bull stance, eyes flat, jaw extended, feet planted wide apart and hands swinging at his sides. Then he happened to glance at Olivia, and saw the radiance in her face. "Guess you neglected to bring your swimming trunks," he said gruffly, taking another look at Grant's navy briefs.

"Among other things." He'd neglected to bring condoms, too, an omission he prayed he wasn't going to live to regret.

"Would you like some coffee, Dad?" Amazingly unperturbed, Olivia lifted the Thermos jug and shook it experimentally. "I think there's another cup left in here."

"I won't bother, thanks. I just stopped by to make

sure you were okay. You disappeared rather suddenly last night.''

''Things were going well enough that I didn't think I'd be missed, and Grant and I wanted to be alone.'' She smiled sunnily. ''In fact, we've seen so little of each other these last few weeks that I'm planning to drive to Vancouver with him when he's finished his tour of duty here.''

The old man went slightly gray around the gills at that bit of news, but, to his credit, he kept a lid on his real feelings. ''Vancouver, eh? That'll take quite some time. How long do you plan to be gone?''

She shrugged. ''A week or two. I haven't had a holiday in three years, so I think I've earned a break.''

A bit concerned by her father's rapid respiration, Grant pulled one of the patio chairs into the shade. ''Why don't you have a seat and get out of the sun, Sam?''

''No, thanks. I've got a ten-thirty tee time at the club.''

''I'll walk you to your car, then,'' he said, heading for the house. ''Give me a minute to find my pants.''

When he came back down, Sam was already halfway to his car. Catching up with him, Grant remarked, ''I know you're not overly thrilled about Olivia driving west with me, and I appreciate your keeping that opinion to yourself.''

''Would it do me any good to air it?''

''No.'' He opened the car door and waited until Sam was settled behind the wheel. ''But that never stopped you before.''

Sam looked up at him the way a snake might regard a mongoose. With utter loathing. ''Don't go throwing your hat in the air too soon. Just because she's agreed to head west with you doesn't mean she's ready to make the move permanent. Her life's here, and she knows it, even if you don't.''

"That's not up to you or me, Sam. She's old enough to make up her own mind."

"Maybe so. But I'll tell you this: you make my girl cry again, Grant Madison, and I'll have your guts for garters."

"I don't aim to do that, Sam."

"You'd better not," Sam said, and drove off in a whirlwind of dust and gravel.

CHAPTER EIGHT

THEY left Springdale eighteen days later, early on the last Thursday in August. Her father, Bethany, and Ingrid from the deli came to see them off. It was a morning of misty sunshine with a hint of fall in the air. Maybe the signs that summer was almost at an end made saying goodbye more melancholy than it otherwise might have been, because Olivia found the moment oddly painful.

Her father had tears in his eyes and hugged her as if he thought he'd never see her again. "Look after yourself, girl."

"You know I will. And don't you forget to take your medication," she said, close to breaking down herself. "I'll phone every few days and let you know where we are."

"Make sure you do." He hugged her again, then somewhat grudgingly turned to Grant and shook his hand. "Good luck and drive carefully. Remember you've got a precious cargo."

Bethany drew her aside as Grant stashed the last of their luggage in the car. "Make it work this time," she whispered. "He's the right man for you, Olivia."

"Don't worry about your dad," Ingrid said. "I'll keep an eye on the old coot. Here, I've brought you a picnic lunch and a couple of snacks to keep you going for the first couple of hundred miles or so. There's nothing worse than some of those fast food joints you'll find along the highway. They'd poison a viper.''

The last thing Olivia saw as the car swept out of the gates was the three of them silhouetted against the bright morning sky, her father with his hand raised in farewell, Bethany waving her hat, and Ingrid planted stolidly between them. Suddenly, she felt as if she'd been cast adrift in a lifeboat without any oars.

''Having second thoughts already?'' Grant inquired, as they headed north out of town, and although he was smiling she sensed that his eyes were watchful behind the dark lenses of his sunglasses.

''How could I be?'' she said. ''The last eight weeks with you have turned my life around. Leaving's a bit of a wrench, I admit, but nothing compared to how I'd be feeling if you were going without me. I guess I just don't like goodbyes.''

''No one does, Liv. I remember the last time I drove away from Springdale, and it was no picnic then, either.''

''I thought you couldn't wait to get away. You'd been so looking forward to your job up north.''

''Because, at the time I applied for it, I'd seen it as a way for you and me to make a fresh start, away from the pressures we faced every day in Springdale. It took some of the shine off the whole venture to discover I'd read the whole situation wrong and you were ready to flush our marriage down the toilet.'' He flung her another enigmatic glance. ''There was many a night I lay awake, wondering if you'd fly up to join me if I sent you a ticket. Would you have, do you think?''

''Probably not,'' she sighed. ''I was angry with you and too caught up in my misery at losing the baby.

The way I saw it, if you really loved me, you wouldn't have wanted to uproot me. I'm ashamed to think I was so selfish.''

"I was pretty selfish myself, Liv, though I didn't realize how much until I landed in Repulse Bay. It was no sort of life up there for a woman like you. In fact, not many women could have handled it. We might have been dedicated doctors, but half the guys I worked with had broken marriages to show for it.''

They'd left the town limits behind by then, and taken the route that would connect them to the Trans-Canada highway snaking up toward Sudbury. The mist had cleared and given way to clear blue skies. Grant opened the sun roof on the car, slipped a CD into the player, and they sang in dreadful harmony to Willie Nelson's 'On The Road Again' as the miles skimmed by and the despondency which had marred the start of their journey melted in the late summer heat.

Around noon, he turned onto a narrow dirt side road and steered the car around the potholes and over the ruts until he found an isolated glade with a creek running through it. They stopped there and ate the picnic lunch Ingrid had prepared: smoked salmon with capers and slivers of red onion on cream cheese and bagels, cherry tomatoes, apple tarts, fresh peaches, and sparkling grape juice.

After, Grant stretched out in the long sweet grass beside the stream, pulled her down beside him and said, "Time for your afternoon nap, sweet face.''

She didn't expect to sleep, but the quiet gurgle of the water and the sun filtering benignly through the canopy of maple branches overhead proved a powerful narcotic. When she awoke, some forty minutes later, Grant had disappeared. She found him wading several yards downstream, where the creek widened into a miniature lake bordered by flat, sun-baked rocks. Shucking off her sandals, she joined him.

"The water's warm as bath water down here, and deep enough to swim in," he said, lacing his fingers through hers. "Feel like taking a dip?"

"I don't have my bathing suit handy."

The look he turned on her was purely lascivious. "I know, Olivia!"

"You surely aren't suggesting…?"

"I surely am," he said, his hands already busy pulling her sleeveless top over her head.

"But someone might see us!"

"They'd have to find us first. We're well screened from the road and there hasn't been a vehicle go by since we got here."

He peeled off his shirt and flung it on the nearest rock. His denim shorts followed, along with his briefs, then, howling like a banshee, he flattened into a shallow dive. "What's it going to be, sweet face?" he yodeled, surfacing and using his arms like windmills to sling handfuls of water at her. "Are you coming in voluntarily, or do I come and get you?"

Since he was determined to soak her to the skin one way or another, it was easier to give in gracefully. Stripping off her own shorts and underwear, she joined him. The water felt divine, smooth as silk and clear as glass, with just enough chill on it to refresh.

"I could get used to horsing around with you," he said, hooking his hands around her neck, "especially when you're dressed like this. It reminds me of when we were first married. Remember how I'd sometimes manage to sneak home between shifts for a little—?"

"Afternoon delight," she finished breathlessly. "I remember."

"Took the words right out of my mouth, Liv," he murmured, pulling her close. "Feel like repeating the experience?"

They'd never made love in eight feet of water before, but they managed beautifully.

In the golden days that followed, she discovered a new Grant, one so relaxed it was difficult relating him to the driven professional she'd married. She had never felt so close to him, so connected. Nor had she ever known such utter contentment or such certainty that this time things were going to work out.

"This is turning into an unforgettable second honeymoon," she told him, the night they stopped at a wonderful old Victorian inn on the shores of Lake Superior. Set in two acres of gardens, with miles of sandy shore in front, it might have been lifted straight from the pages of a country lifestyle magazine.

They'd eaten dinner on the wrap-around porch, feasting on chilled crayfish salad followed by quail in a potato torte with juniper berries, and had decided on a stroll along the beach before turning in.

"It's got to be an improvement over the first," he said wryly. "All you got then was a night in the bridal suite at The Ambassador in Springdale."

"It's not where we are that makes the difference, Grant. It's the fact that this time around we're having fun."

"Yeah." He sifted his bare feet through the fine white sand. "'Fun' isn't exactly the word I'd use to describe our marriage. We did too much fighting and not nearly enough laughing. And you, sweetheart," he said, swinging her around to face him and tracing his forefinger down her cheek, "did too much crying. If I haven't said it before, I want to tell you now that I'm sorry for that."

Another night, they stayed in Manitoba, in a small hotel lifted straight out of a 1930s movie set overlooking the Red River valley, and ate Winnipeg goldeye washed down with their host's homemade rhubarb wine. It was a side of Canada Olivia had never seen before and she found it enchanting. Springdale seemed a million miles away.

They were crossing southern Saskatchewan when they came on the accident. A car had blown a tire and rolled into the ditch. As Grant pulled up behind it, a man was helping a woman lift a child clear of the wreckage.

Grant swore, reached for the medical bag he kept on the back seat and pulled his cellphone from its pocket on the console. "Here, Liv, call for help, then come and give me a hand. It'll take a while for an ambulance to get here, so we're in for a little frontier first-aid. Are you up to it?"

She'd never been good with anything to do with blood, but neither was she willing to turn her back on someone needing help. "I'm up to it," she said.

The man and his wife had been wearing seat belts, and so had escaped serious injury, but the child had been sleeping on the back seat and been flung forward by the impact. He was unconscious and bleeding from a head wound.

When Olivia joined them, Grant had taken charge. The boy was stretched out on the dry yellow grass beside the road, covered by a blanket the man had produced from the overturned vehicle. The woman ran back and forth, wringing her hands and moaning.

"This cut needs cleaning before it's treated," Grant said, examining the child closely. "Olivia, there are gauze packs at the bottom of my bag, and antiseptic. And hand me my stethoscope while you're at it, then for pity's sake try to calm the mother."

She did her best, offering comfort to the poor woman who fluttered helplessly around her son, weeping uncontrollably and asking if he was going to die. "No," Olivia assured her, and prayed she was right.

"He's only seven," the mother sobbed. "Just a little boy, and all we have."

The father simply stood there, almost vacant with shock. "Come and sit down, both of you," Olivia urged. "Your son's in very good hands. My husband's a doctor."

My husband's a doctor.... She'd never before spoken the words with such pride; that she could make the claim now, when only the doctor part was strictly true, struck her as cruelly ironic. When their marriage had most needed support, she'd seen his profession as an adversary, the "other woman" with whom he'd preferred to spend his time.

"How is he?" she asked in a low voice, going over to where he knelt beside the still-unconscious child.

"It's a nasty gash and he's knocked himself out cold, though I doubt he's fractured his skull. Head injuries are funny things, though, and he needs a more thorough check at a hospital once we've done what we can here. Is an ambulance on its way?"

"Yes, but it's coming from forty miles away so we're facing a bit of a wait."

"That's okay. His vital signs are good and he's in no immediate danger. Look, Liv, if you wouldn't mind trying to keep the wound clear of blood while I suture him up, I can get the job done faster. Then, if you'll keep an eye on him, I want to give the parents the once-over."

"How are they doing?" she asked, when he returned.

"They're a bit shocky, which is to be expected, but otherwise okay. More to the point, how's this little guy making out?"

He stooped over the child and she saw the gentleness in his touch as he handled the boy, and his patience with the parents as they fretted about their son's injury and the length of time it was taking for him to be shipped to a hospital.

"That could have been our son," Grant said, when they resumed their journey. "He'd be about seven by now. Do you ever wonder what he'd have been like?"

"Not as often any more. But I used to. For years after the miscarriage, I daydreamed about how he'd have been."

"Me, too, though my concern came a bit too late to be of any comfort to you. I behaved like an ass."

It was the first time in days that they'd talked about that sad era. Most of the time, they focused on the future. But as they traversed the vast wheat fields of south-eastern Alberta he told her about the years after he'd left the medevac team in Repulse Bay. "I got the wandering bug out of my system. Enough days holed up in the back of a hut or trailer in the middle of the frozen wilds tends to tame a man and make him more appreciative of the finer comforts in life.

When the offer came up to complete a cardiology residency in California, I was ready for it.''

''When did you come back to Canada?''

''Six months ago. I've been subbing for doctors in the Vancouver area—women on maternity leave, people going on vacation, that kind of thing. But now I've been offered a post at one of the best hospitals in Vancouver and I'm pretty sure I'll take it.''

He flung her a sideways glance and grinned. ''It'll be a mortgage and a house in the suburbs next. Bet you never thought I'd become so domesticated, did you?''

''No,'' she said. ''I never did. You were always such a gypsy.''

''Yeah. That made it tough on you, I know. You paid the price for my having been tied to a dingy two-room apartment in Toronto all through my boyhood. How I used to envy the other kids I knew who spent the summers at summer camp, out at the lake! But for there to have been enough money for that kind of thing in our house would have meant my dad had to get off his idle butt and go to work. My mom did her best, but when you're the only one putting food on the table and paying the rent, there isn't a lot left over for extras.''

''How is your mother?'' Olivia asked. ''You've hardly mentioned her since you came back.''

''She's great. Living it up with her sister down on the Niagara Peninsula. She won a bundle on the lottery about a year after my father died, and is comfortably off for the first time in her life, so she and my aunt travel quite a bit, especially in the winter.''

Olivia thought of the recently widowed mother-in-law she'd met the day before her wedding. Tall, thin and soberly dressed, Jane Madison had been a lonely figure among the more elegantly clad Whitfield guests who'd filled the church and danced the night away at the Country Club after the ceremony. "I wish I'd gotten to know her better. We only met a couple of times."

"One thing at a time, Liv," Grant said. "Let's not rush our fences. It's early days yet."

But it wasn't, not the way Olivia saw things. Even allowing for leisurely driving, they'd reach Vancouver in another three or four days. Once there, she'd spend perhaps another week getting to know something of the city, then it would be time for her to fly home. What if it proved not time enough for them to commit to a future together? How well would either of them tolerate a long-distance courtship?

He squeezed her knee. "Don't look so down. There's no statute of limitations in effect here, sweetheart. So far, things are going well. Better than well, in fact. But the last thing either of us wants is to have another marriage blow up in our faces, so be patient."

He spoke of marriage as if it were a very real possibility, yet for all their recent closeness he'd never once told her he loved her, and she, after that one time by her pool, had not repeated the words to him because she knew him too well. Behind the laughter and the sharing and the intimacy lay a lingering caution, as if he were waiting for old bad habits to resurface. If she pressed too hard, before he was ready, he'd pull away from her. Her experience seven years earlier had taught her that much.

"So where are we stopping tonight?" she said, determined not to let pessimism spoil what had, so far, been an idyllic holiday.

By way of answer, he pointed to the western horizon, where the outline of tall buildings rose against the evening sky. "There," he said. "That's Calgary. And when you wake up tomorrow, you'll be able to look out of our hotel window and see the Rockies. Tomorrow we'll have lunch in Banff, and tomorrow night…" He leered charmingly. "Tomorrow night, my darling, I have a special treat in store. Hope you packed one of those drop-dead-gorgeous dresses in your suitcase because you're going to need it."

If diverting her had been his plan, it had worked. For the next two hours, she tried to weasel the secret out of him. She didn't succeed, but the exercise lifted her spirits.

"So," he said, coming up behind her as she stood at their hotel room window late the next afternoon and gazed at the view. "Was it worth the suspense?"

She swallowed, overwhelmed on all fronts. Seven storeys below shimmered a perfect oval of glacier-fed aquamarine water ringed by majestic mountains. Behind her, the old-world ambience and elegance of the Château Lake Louise enfolded her in the luxury of the suite he'd reserved for them for the next three nights. Bouquets of flowers, champagne on ice, a basket of fruit, thick terry robes, huge velvet-piled towels, and an array of bath toiletries to please a queen— the list went on and on.

"I've never seen anything so lovely," she whispered. "This place, the mountains, the lake—they're magical!"

"I wish I could have brought you here on our wedding night, sweetheart," he said, pulling her back to lean against his chest and kissing the top of her head.

''It's what you deserved. But we're here now, and I want to make up for what you missed the first time around.''

They'd made love many times, in many places, over the last week, but nothing came close to what they shared in the hour that followed. Dipping his finger in his champagne glass, he traced the veins running along her inner arms and over her breasts. With his tongue, he toured the arch of her instep, the hollow at the back of her knees. He charted a path from her earlobes to her navel, from her breasts to her thighs to the small of her back.

And she—oh, she practiced her own subtle torture, running her hand up the length of his long legs and stopping just short of where his flesh proclaimed itself more than willing to accommodate her.

She wanted to pleasure him as he'd pleasured her, with uninhibited dedication, kissing him all over, tasting him.... She hesitated, and ran her tongue over her lips, unsure if she dared...she never had before...would he be shocked if...?

She sneaked a glance at him, saw the smile touching his mouth, the laughing awareness in his eyes. ''You wouldn't!'' he taunted softly.

''Yes, I would,'' she said breathlessly and, bending her head, skimmed her tongue over one nipple and the flat hard plane of his belly, and took him in her mouth.

His initial gasp of startled pleasure soon disintegrated into a plea for mercy. She had not known she could be so bold, and gloried in her power over him.

But he was not easily subdued, and quickly gained the upper hand again. ''You taste of wild honey,'' he muttered hoarsely, staring down at her where she writhed against him in shameless abandon.

In a frenzy to have him possess her completely, to feel him touching and filling every corner and crevice that made up her being, she reached for him. "Come into me," she begged. "Come *with* me!"

And when he did, the low, slow thunder he'd aroused built in her blood to a roaring tumult and left her steeped in the aftermath of a passion she'd only ever known with him and had never wanted to recreate with any other man. He was her heart, her soul. He was, and always would be, her life.

Smiling and sated, she fell into a light doze, only semi-aware of him leaving her side to climb into his clothes. She murmured sleepily as he kissed her ear and told her he had an errand to run, half heard the door close behind him, and didn't know another thing until she opened her eyes an hour later to find the room swathed in shadows and Grant leaning over her, his expression so full of pent-up emotion that she wondered how she could begin to doubt his love.

Reaching up, she grabbed him around the neck and brought him toppling down beside her. "This bed," she sighed, "is much too big for one."

Later, while she lazed up to her chin in scented bubbles, he sat on the edge of the marble bath tub and fed her strawberries and champagne. "You're spoiling me," she sighed, reveling in his attentions.

"I'm making up for lost time, sweetheart."

"But I want to do special things for you, too."

"You already have, Liv. You're here, and that's more than enough." He stood up and stretched. "I've got a special evening planned, so I'm off to shave and shower. Try to behave while I'm gone, woman.''

"What possible mischief could I get up to?'' she said, all manner of delightful options springing to mind.

"With your insatiable appetite, anything's possible, and the shower in the other bathroom's plenty big enough for two." He eyed her severely. "But unless you want me carried out of here on a stretcher, you'll restrain yourself until I've had a chance to recharge my battery.''

"Well, heaven forbid anything should impair the function of your battery!'' she cooed, batting her lashes at him.

He had something special planned. Could that possibly mean...?

Don't! she admonished herself, scrubbing shampoo into her hair, then rinsing it clean with the handheld shower spray. *Don't go wishing for the moon when you already have so much. Just do and be your best for him.*

Wrapping herself in one of the big, velvety bath sheets, she dried her hair, then sat at the vanity to begin the feminine rituals that are part and parcel of every woman's repertoire when it comes to pleasing her man. A hint of glittery green on her eyelids to bring out the jade specks in her eyes, a coat of mascara on her lashes, a sweep of blusher to highlight her cheekbones, pale rose lip gloss, and a subtle aura of designer perfume at her throat and wrists and behind her knees. And finally her hair, swept up on top of her head in a gleaming coil.

She chose cool black satin underwear extravagantly trimmed in French lace, gossamer-fine stockings the color of nightshade, and finished off the ensemble with a simple black dress and black silk pumps. Apart from a gold bangle, which had been her mother's, her only jewelry was a pair of small diamond stud earrings which Grant had given her as a wedding present.

Although she hadn't worn them in seven years, she'd kept them for sentimental reasons, along with her wedding band and diamond solitaire engagement ring. When he'd invited her to drive across Canada with him, she'd taken the earrings out of her safety deposit box and tucked them in a side pocket of her overnight bag in the superstitious hope that, if the opportunity to wear them happened to arise, perhaps the rings might also see the light of day again before too long.

Would he remember them and recognize their significance? she wondered, taking a last look in the mirrored closet doors. Or was she allowing too much to hinge on inconsequentials, as she had the night of the Sunflower Ball?

Shaking her head at her own foolishness, she went into the sitting room to wait for Grant. The sun had gone down, leaving the glacier glowing icily in the twilight and the lake lying pale and calm beneath a honeydew-colored sky. If proof that he was committed to making things work out between them this time was what she was looking for, she surely had the evidence spread out around her in this idyllic setting.

"You about ready to roll, Liv?" he called from the dressing room off the bedroom. "It's only just past seven, and our dinner reservation isn't for another hour, but I want to go down early and take you down to the lakefront before we eat."

His mention of the time reminded her that it was

almost nine in Springdale and that she hadn't phoned her father in several days. She'd be leaving it too late to call him after dinner, and she knew how he looked forward to hearing from her.

"Sounds lovely, Grant. Give me five minutes, and I'll be ready," she said, and lifted the receiver off the hook.

He knew the minute he walked into the sitting room that something had happened to change things, and that whatever it was he wasn't going to like it. She stood by the desk, her face stripped of color. "Hey," he said, removing the phone dangling from her hand and replacing it. "What's up?"

"It's my father," she said hollowly.

A chunk of dread thumped into the pit of his stomach. Had he really needed to ask? Of course it was Sam. Everything *always* came back to Sam!

"What about him, Liv?" he said, striving to keep his tone neutral.

"He's…had some sort of setback with his heart."

Uh-huh! "Setback" was a good word, calculated to generate a sympathetic response without being too medically specific. "That's what he called it? A setback?"

"No. Edward answered the phone and he's the one who told me."

Nice move, getting the faithful old family retainer to do the dirty work! Sam hadn't lost his touch!

"He didn't even want to put my call through, except Dad insisted on speaking to me, and…oh, Grant!" She turned to him, her eyes wide and tragic. "He sounded so weak."

"But not too ill to take a phone call." He almost

choked on the uprush of rage that consumed him. "That should tell you something, Liv."

She shook her head and, despite her high heels, fairly sprinted into the bedroom. "No! If I hadn't known who it was, I wouldn't have recognized his voice."

Following at a deliberately measured pace, he found she'd already hauled her suitcase onto the luggage rack. "What are you doing, Olivia?" he said, wondering how the hell he could coat the question in ice when he was on fire inside.

"Isn't it obvious?" she said. "I'm packing. I'll have to fly home."

The rage burned a little brighter, if that was possible. "What's obvious to me is that you're overreacting. Before you go racing off half-cocked, consider this: if Sam's condition were serious, he'd be hospitalized. The fact that he's not should be of some comfort."

"You didn't hear him," she said, flinging clothes haphazardly into the suitcase. "If you had, you'd understand."

He understood all too well. "Listen to me," he snapped, grabbing her by the shoulders and forcing her to stop the ridiculous, headlong rush into panic. "You're going way over the top here. At the very least, wait until morning before you make any decision about going home. Let me talk to Edward. Better yet, let me talk to Sam's doctor and get the facts."

But she wasn't hearing him. "I should have phoned more often," she wailed. "I hadn't spoken to him in nearly four days. Perhaps if I had, I'd have seen this coming."

"Yeah, well, that'll do it every time," he said

scornfully, frustration getting the better of his judgment. "It's well documented that lack of frequent telephone contact will bring on myocardial infarction, especially in control freaks like Sam Whitfield."

"Are you suggesting he's...*faking* illness?"

The look she turned on him made him feel knee-high to a grasshopper, but he plowed on regardless. "I wouldn't put it past him. He's tried just about everything else to keep us apart."

"I can't believe you said that, Grant," she said in a shocked whisper. "I thought we'd got past this kind of rubbish."

"I'll be more than happy to apologize if I'm doing him an injustice."

"But you don't think you are, do you?"

He shrugged and turned away, unable to meet the accusation and hurt in her eyes. "Describe his symptoms again. Tell me exactly what he said."

"*He* didn't say anything. I already explained that Edward's the one who told me. All my father wanted to know was if I'm happy and...when I thought I'd be coming home."

"Exactly." He swung back to face her. "Do you see a pattern here, Olivia?"

"I don't know," she cried, tears washing out of her eyes and streaking her cheeks with make-up. "I only know I have to decide what to do next and I need you to help me."

"Then I will," he said. "It's pretty straightforward, really. Make a choice, Olivia. Who do you trust the most, your father or me?"

CHAPTER NINE

"YOU don't understand! This isn't about who I love the most or where I want to be," she said, her pupils huge in her pale face. "It's about an old man who could be dying. It's about my father. If it were your mother, I wouldn't ask you to choose. I wouldn't give you ultimatums. I'd be there for you, *with* you."

"I'm not suggesting you abandon him, Olivia. All I'm asking is that you wait and get the facts from his doctors before you go charging off to be by his side."

"You think he's lying," she said. "Admit it. You think he's deliberately trying to sabotage our holiday."

"I think he's capable of that, yes."

"And you might be right. Heaven knows, he can be manipulative when he puts his mind to it—"

Grant laughed bitterly. "That's the understatement of the century!"

"But the only way I can be sure is to go home and see for myself." She appealed to him with outstretched hands. "That's all I'm asking, Grant: a few days to put my mind at rest. As soon as I know he's going to be all right, I'll fly out and meet you in Vancouver."

"No," he said flatly. "If you choose to leave now, forget about coming back. I let him talk you out of our marriage seven years ago, but I'm damned if I'll put up with that kind of interference again."

She sighed. "In case you haven't noticed, we're no longer married."

"We could be," he said. "If I were convinced you'd matured enough to sever your ties to Springdale, that you were willing to trust my judgment for a change, we could be married sooner than you think."

"No, we couldn't!" she cried. "I'm not blind, and I'm not the naive little fool you used to know, and I won't let you exploit the situation like this! Ever since we left Springdale, you've been watching me the way a cat watches a mouse, waiting for me to make a mistake. Waiting for me to prove that you were right the first time and I'm just not made of the right stuff to be the almighty Dr. Madison's chosen mate."

"And I wasn't far off the mark, was I? One call home and before you've even hung up the phone our whole relationship starts circling the drain again because I don't see matters the way you do."

"In case you haven't noticed," she said, planting her fists on her hips and glaring at him, "trust breeds trust. And that means both parties have to be willing to take risks and believe in the other. But the bottom line is that you aren't, Grant. I've given you everything I have, everything I am—every last piece of my heart, all my love—and it's still not enough!" She dashed at her eyes, her momentary flash of anger drowned out in a fresh spate of tears. "I must have been mad to think it ever would be."

"That's the trouble with you, Olivia," he said cuttingly. "You're always so ready to give. Problem is, when you don't get your own way, you snatch it all back again."

Her face closed, wiping itself clean of all expression. "I guess there isn't any more to say, then, is there? I'll finish packing and make arrangements to rent a car to get to the nearest airport."

"Forget it," he said, tired suddenly of the whole bloody mess and wanting it to be over, once and for all. "You're in no shape to be out on the road by yourself. I'll drive you to Calgary first thing in the morning."

"And what do you propose we do between now and then?" she asked stonily. "Spend the night together in the same bed? Thanks anyway, but I'll pass. In any case, I want to be on the first flight east tomorrow morning."

"Fine, then!" He threw up his hands in surrender. "Whatever you say, duchess. We'll do it your way, as usual, and the sooner the better. It won't take me long to throw my stuff together. We can be on the road in twenty minutes and in Calgary within three hours."

"I appreciate the offer, but there's really no need for you to cut short your stay here just because my plans have changed," she said piously, scooping up an armful of frothy underwear and tossing it in her suitcase. "You've gone to so much trouble, booking this suite and all, it's ridiculous to let it go to waste."

He thought of the evening he had planned, of the emerald and diamond dinner ring he'd bought at the jewelry shop in the hotel lobby while she'd napped that afternoon, and which he'd stashed in the breast pocket of his suit jacket before he woke her and they made love again.

It wasn't the most expensive ring, but it would have served the purpose until they got to Vancouver and he could choose a really good diamond, something she'd want to wear for the rest of her life—unlike the pitiful chip of a stone which was all he'd been able to afford the first time they'd gotten engaged.

He'd intended to propose down by the lake, with only the stars and a sliver of new moon as witnesses. He'd arranged a special table in the dining room, a special meal, special wines. He'd planned to dance with her, to make the evening one she'd always remember.

Hell, the way it had turned out, neither of them were ever likely to forget it!

"This might come as a surprise, sweet face," he sneered, spreading his arm in a sweeping gesture to encompass the whole suite, "but all this trouble I went to was for *us,* not me."

A ray of hope lit up her features. "Then put everything on hold for a few days."

He was tempted, no question of that. It would be easy enough to bury his doubts, salvage what was left of today with the placebo of a ring and a proposal, and direct his hopes and energy on next week, or next month, or whenever she might see fit to remember they might have a future together.

The thing was, what if she didn't? What if, at the end of it all, he picked up the phone one night to hear her tell him she wasn't interested after all?

He'd spent the better part of a year wondering if she was as full of regret for their failed marriage as he'd been, if she, too, lay awake at night, wondering where he was, if he was happy, if she ever thought of him. He'd got his answer one bitter November afternoon, when she served him with divorce papers. He wasn't prepared to go down that road again.

"I don't think so, Olivia. I'm not that much of a devil for punishment."

"I thought we were going to make things work this time," she mourned, biting her lips to keep from crying out loud. "I really thought that we were among the lucky ones who get a second chance."

He turned away from the sight of her pain, too consumed with his own. "Miracles seldom happen outside fairy tales, Olivia."

It seemed to her that everyone in the hotel saw their departure and knew that the couple who'd arrived radiant with happiness only a few hours before were leaving under a cloud of misery. She saw the desk clerk's discreetly raised eyebrows, the porter's sympathetic rush to hold open the door for her, and the way he kindly avoided making eye contact with her so that they could both pretend her face wasn't swollen from weeping.

No one could have mistaken Grant's actions as anything other than those of a man seething with suppressed rage. White around the mouth, nostrils pinched, eyes as cold and dead as flint, he stalked through the lobby of the hotel and out into the parking area with the grim stoicism of someone about to face a firing squad.

"I'd really just as soon drive myself," she said, when he pulled the car up in front of the main hotel entrance.

"Shut up and get in," he said, "and let's get this over with."

The journey to Calgary continued the nightmare. He slouched against the arm rest on the door, as far away from her as he could get short of hopping into the back seat and driving from there. Once clear of the resort area, he leaned back and pressed down on the accelerator as if the hounds of hell were in pursuit.

They passed the picnic area where they'd stopped just the day before and followed a trail under the trees, searching for a place where they could be alone because they hadn't made love since that morning and couldn't wait a minute longer.

The reality of knowing she'd never again inhale the sweet, dusty scent of wild grass or the intense resinous tang of pine trees without thinking of him stabbed her more cruelly than a knife in the heart.

Just after ten o'clock, he pulled into an all-night hamburger stand somewhere the other side of Banff. "I'm picking up a coffee and something to eat," he said. "You want anything?"

Yes, she thought sadly. *I want you. But if this is the best we can do when trouble shows its face, I'm going to have to learn to live without you.* "No, thanks. I couldn't eat a thing."

He shrugged. "Suit yourself," he said indifferently.

Would he even notice if she slipped out of the car while his back was turned? she wondered, wishing the night would just swallow her up whole and spare her having to live out the rest of her miserable days.

Too soon, they reached the outskirts of Calgary. In the strobe-like glare of streetlights flashing through the car, she stole another look at his profile. He might have been carved in granite.

Sensing her gaze, he asked, "You have any particular motel in mind where you want to spend the night?"

As if she could sleep a wink! "No," she said. "Just

drop me off at the airport. I'll be comfortable enough in the executive lounge until morning.''

''Always assuming it's staffed around the clock for the convenience of people like you, of course.''

''If it's not, I'll find some other place to wait. I'm quite capable of surviving the night on the floor in the main lobby if I have to, so please don't feel you have to worry about me, Grant.''

''I don't,'' he said. ''All that came to an end when you decided you'd rather go rushing back home than stay with me.''

Oh, she could have slapped him for his stubborn, punitive, childish refusal to compromise or try to see her point of view! ''Much more of listening to that kind of talk, and I'll be as glad to see the back of you as you clearly are of me,'' she snapped.

But when it came to saying goodbye, she fell apart. The tears she'd thought she'd exhausted flooded her eyes anew, blinding her when she most needed to see him clearly enough to imprint on her memory the image of his dark, level eyebrows, the thick sweep of his lashes, the passionate, angry curve of his mouth, the intractable line of his jaw.

Stifling a sob, she reached for him. He caught her hands and trapped them against her chest. ''No,'' he said hoarsely, pushing her away. ''Try playing fair, for a change.''

''I love you,'' she said, her heart breaking.

''Yeah,'' he said. ''Just not enough, though, sweet face.''

A minute later, she was alone, with her suitcases and overnight bag at her feet and nothing inside her but a great gaping wound full of broken dreams.

* * *

She'd been home about three weeks when Bethany showed up at the front door one Saturday morning. "I only just heard you were back," she said. "How come you're hiding away in here? What's going on?"

Olivia closed the folder she'd been working on and combed her fingers through her hair. "Nothing. I came home early because Dad suffered a mild heart attack, and once he was out of the woods, I had to get busy finalizing sponsors for the Christmas Sale."

"Yes. And?"

"Nothing."

"Quit stonewalling, Olivia! What happened with you and Grant? Why isn't he here with you?"

"He had a job waiting in Vancouver."

Silence ticked by for several minutes while Bethany digested that piece of news. Finally, she said, "Go put some shoes on. We're going out for lunch."

"No," Olivia said. "Thanks anyway, but not today."

"We're going out for lunch, Olivia, and I'm not taking no for an answer."

She waited until they'd been shown to a quiet corner in the Riverside Room at The Ambassador Hotel and ordered shrimp omelets before fixing Olivia in the sort of don't-mess-with-me stare she directed with such effect at her students. "Okay, what gives? And if you say 'nothing' one more time, so help me I'll scream and bring everyone in this mausoleum running to see what's going on."

"Things didn't work out between me and Grant," Olivia said.

"I already figured that out for myself. What I want to know is how you managed to screw up when you had such a good thing going."

Olivia stared listlessly out of the window. Already the maple trees along the river valley were turning red. Pretty soon it would be Thanksgiving, and then Christmas, and before she knew it, another year would have rolled by. How many more, before the pain came to an end? "It takes two to make a relationship tick, Beth. You know that."

"Oh, damn!" Bethany touched the back of her hand contritely. "I'm sorry. I didn't mean to come on so strong. It's just that I really thought he was the right man for you."

"So did I, but what I had to offer wasn't enough for him," Olivia said, fighting to swallow the lump in her throat which was her constant companion these days. "He wanted to be the *only* man. With him, it's a clear-cut case of black or white, with no gray bits in between—a straightforward choice between him and my father. He doesn't understand I've got room in my heart for both."

"So call him up and set him straight. Better yet, go out there and explain it to him in person. Men can be pretty dense at times."

"No," she said, pushing aside her barely touched omelet. "He made it pretty clear he wasn't interested in hearing anything I had to say."

"Then let him stew in his own juice for a while. Maybe when he's had time to reflect a bit he'll be more inclined to listen to reason, because, from everything I saw, he's as besotted with you as you are with him. Meanwhile, eat up. There's nothing to be gained by starving yourself and you look like hell."

But she hadn't had an appetite in days, and seemed to be feeding on her own misery, instead. Try as she might, she couldn't get the picture out of her mind of how Grant had looked at the Calgary airport. Wounded and betrayed and so remote there had been no reaching him. "Some things can't be fixed," he'd said, when she'd begged him one last time to reconsider his position.

"I'm not hungry," she told Bethany now. "To be honest, food almost makes me sick just lately."

Bethany regarded her sharply. "I'd suggest we go back to your place and get roaring drunk, but you're so straight-arrow you'd chicken out before we'd half finished the first bottle of wine. So I'm going to give you another shot of unasked-for advice, instead. Don't give up on that man without a fight, Olivia. He's too good a specimen to chuck out with the rest of the garbage."

"It's too late for that," Olivia said. "We've done too much damage."

"It's never too late," Bethany scoffed. "At least, not as long as you've still got breath left in your body. There's too much potential for either of you to give up on rebuilding."

Her plea didn't fall on completely deaf ears. There'd been many a time in the last weeks when Olivia had picked up the phone to call him, and even more times when it had rung and she'd raced to answer, spurred by hope that he might have softened his attitude. Her head might be telling her it was all over between them, but her heart didn't want to believe it. There came a point, though, when a person had to accept what couldn't be changed and simply move forward on her own.

"What's the point in rebuilding," she said to Bethany, "if, at the first sign of trouble, he tears it all down again? It's as if he's determined not to let anyone else beat him to the punch.''

"Go to him, Olivia. Make him believe you're in this for the long haul. Stop letting him punish himself and you.''

She mulled over the idea, and came very close to acting on it—until the day her GP told her the reason she couldn't stay awake past nine at night or keep her breakfast down had nothing to do with stress and everything to do with being nearly two months pregnant.

The news hit Olivia like a sudden attack of the flu, bowling her over and leaving her trembling with fever. Her stomach lurched and rolled, a flush rode up her body, her head felt light.

"I'm surprised you haven't already figured it out for yourself,'' her doctor said, in the face of her reaction. "It's not as though this is your first experience.''

"But I didn't have any of these symptoms before! It just never occurred to me....''

"Well, every pregnancy's different, and possibly the embryo wasn't well implanted with the first and that's why you didn't go full term. But everything's looking good this time around.'' He peered at her over the top of her chart. "I take it that's welcome news, Olivia?''

"Yes,'' she said, still shaken. "Why would you think otherwise?''

"You obviously didn't plan on a baby and there's no husband in sight. Some might see those as reasons to terminate—''

Get rid of Grant's baby? "No!'' she exclaimed. "My situation might not be ideal right now, but I'd never choose an abortion. I'll cope, one way or the other.''

But it would have to be without her child's father, she realized sadly, as the full impact of what this latest development meant hit home. He'd been resentful enough the first time she'd told him she was pregnant, and she'd been his wife at the time.

"You did this on purpose to bring me in line!" he'd accused her.

"It takes two, Grant," she'd said, appalled at how angry he was, and hurt that he'd think her capable of using an innocent baby to further her own ends.

"But you're the one on the pill. If it was too much trouble to take the damned thing, why didn't you say so? There are other means of contraception.''

"It happened over New Year's," she'd tried to explain. "Remember how we decided on the spur of the moment to take off for the weekend? We left in such a hurry, I forgot...."

He'd seared her with such a look she'd been unable to finish the sentence. In retrospect, her excuse had sounded so pitifully feeble that it was small wonder he'd refused to accept it.

"I might as well save my breath this time, too," she told Bethany, later that day. "The only time we didn't use a condom was the weekend of the Sunflower Ball. He wanted to wait but I'd had enough, and..."

"And when a woman sets her mind on seducing a man, he doesn't have a snowball's chance in hell," Bethany finished. "You don't need to spell it out for me, Olivia. I've been there myself and I get the picture. But that doesn't mean you can't share the news

with him now. You never know, he might see this as
a way to back down gracefully.''

"More likely he'll blame me and accuse me of trying to force his hand.''

"Oh, get over yourself, for crying out loud! Having
a man's child is about something more important than
blame! You talk about his pride being bigger than
both of you, but right now it's yours that's getting in
the way.''

Again, the words struck home, and Olivia felt herself weakening. He had the right to know, after all,
and if she made it clear when she told him that she
wasn't expecting anything from him that he didn't
want to give, might he not soften his attitude?
"Maybe I'll call him tonight,'' she said.

Bethany snorted contemptuously. "Instead of taking the easy way out, why don't you hop on a plane
and tell him to his face? At least that way he can't
hang up on you.''

She almost did that, and even got as far as booking
her flight. Then, the night before she was due to leave,
her father had another heart attack, and this time it
was more than just a warning. It was serious enough
that no one was willing to predict his chances of surviving it.

Winter came early to Vancouver that year, with gray
skies, drizzle, soggy leaves underfoot, and mist ob-
scuring the mountains most days. It matched Grant's
mood in a way he could have done without. He hadn't
expected it would take more than a week or two to
get himself back on track after the fiasco of Lake
Louise. How many times, after all, did a man need to
repeat a mistake before he learned his lesson?

But Thanksgiving came and went without any relief. As October slid into November and the pre-Christmas social season kicked into gear, he dated other women—nice, uncomplicated women, eager to please and with no excess baggage hanging around to screw things up. But when a man was used to the spice and bite of exotic food, plain old white bread wasn't enough to satisfy him. And Olivia, whatever else her shortcomings, had been all the spice he'd needed to make life interesting.

He drove himself mercilessly, working so many extra shifts that the head nurse in Emergency wanted to know if he'd taken up permanent residence in the hospital. She wasn't far off the mark, because the penthouse apartment had lost its appeal. He felt disgruntled enough, without looking out on a seascape of watery grays and people scurrying along the sidewalks, heads bent against the blustery winds of autumn.

They all had places to go. Warm places. With someone waiting at the door to welcome them home. All he had were memories he wished he could shed, but they clung to him like a sickness.

He carried the picture with him all the time, of Olivia as she'd looked the last time he'd seen her: all frozen, damp-eyed misery and hurt. She haunted him, following him along the silent halls of the hospital at midnight, down the aisles of the supermarket when he thought to stock up his empty refrigerator, through the heart of downtown on a busy Saturday afternoon.

He was reminded of her at every turn: in a lovely face peering out from a passing bus, a deliciously leggy woman crossing the street, a young mother in Stanley Park on a rare sunny day in early December.

He saw her everywhere, and found her nowhere. He ached for her and fed on his hatred for Sam, who'd stolen her away from him a second time, because anger was easier to stomach than emptiness. Over Christmas, he worked three days straight, then dragged himself home, finally exhausted enough to sleep the clock around.

He'd have continued in that vein until he dropped, had Justin Greer not phoned him early one morning in January and given him reason to snap out of it.

"You set on staying in Vancouver?" Justin wanted to know, once they'd got past the preliminaries.

"No," he said. "I'm no longer so sure of anything much."

"Good," Justin said. "Because I've got something more tempting to offer. How'd you like to take over as second-in-command of cardiology at Springdale General? I've got my hands full with my private practice and I want to spend more time with Val. After the job you did here last summer, you'd be a shoe-in as my replacement, if you're interested."

"With Sam Whitfield calling the shots? I don't think so! But thanks for thinking of me."

The sudden pause at the other end of the line would have had him wondering if they'd been cut off, except he could hear announcements coming over a public address system in the background. When Justin finally cut back in again, there was a caginess in his voice that hadn't been there a minute earlier. "I assumed you'd heard," he said. "Sam's no longer chairman of the board. He retired last fall."

"And the hospital's still running without him? Gee, imagine that!"

"Actually, the new chairman's the one who put

your name forward for this job. You come pretty highly recommended, pal, and I thought…well, given the situation with Olivia and all.…''

He'd steeled himself not to ask, but when the opportunity to do so landed practically in his lap, he couldn't resist. ''Ah, yes, Olivia,'' he said offhandedly. ''How's she doing, anyway?''

Again, that hollow echo funneled down the line before Justin answered. ''About as well as you'd expect, given her changed circumstances.''

''You've lost me,'' Grant said, some weird inner radar suddenly giving off signals that had the hair standing up on the back of his neck. ''What changed circumstances?''

''You mean, you don't know?''

''Quit stalling, Justin. If I knew, I wouldn't be asking! Olivia and I haven't…been in touch for some time. Did she decide to marry The Suit, is that it?''

Justin broke into a laugh, the kind that just sort of coughs out when somebody else says something incredibly stupid and embarrassing. ''She's pregnant, man!''

Grant went so cold he could barely get his next words out. ''How far along?''

''Around five months, I'd guess. Enough that it's no secret around town, certainly.''

''And The Suit's not…in the picture?''

''Nobody's in the picture, Grant, unless you count her father. She moved back in with him a couple of months ago.''

Well, wasn't that cosy! Sam had her back under his roof where he could keep tabs on her and get his hooks into his grandchild. He must be laughing himself sick at the coup he'd pulled off!

But not for long! A guy didn't have to be a math genius to add up, and that was *his* baby she was carrying. And he'd see Sam Whitfield in hell before he'd let him raise his child. As for Olivia...he'd have a few choice words for her, too, the next time he saw her! Did she really think she could get away with not telling him that he'd fathered another baby? Was this her way of paying him back for the last time?

Yanking the phone off the bedside table, he carried it to the window. The sun was just coming up and flashing silver off a jet heading northwest across the Georgia Strait. "Maybe I'm interested in that job, after all," he told Justin. "I'll call and set up an interview."

CHAPTER TEN

WHEN Edward announced, one Saturday morning in January, that she had a visitor waiting in the library, Olivia assumed it was Bethany, who usually stopped by on the weekend to check on the progress of her future godchild. Olivia looked forward to those visits; they kept her going when other worries threatened to overwhelm her.

"Hi," she said, halting in the doorway while her eyes adjusted to the dazzle of sun streaming into the room. Two days before, a storm had dumped almost a foot of fresh snow on Springdale and its reflected glare was blinding. "I'm so glad you dropped in, Beth. I've got the first baby picture to show you. Can you stay for coff—?"

But the figure silhouetted against the long window was, she realized belatedly, too tall and too broad to be Bethany. And the voice...dear heaven, she could have picked out that voice in a crowd of hundreds! "How are you, Olivia?" he purred, with exquisite courtesy.

"Rather pregnant," she replied baldly, shock and the fact that she'd more or less let the cat out of the bag anyway rendering her incapable of prevaricating.

"So I see. Congratulations to all three of you."

"All...three?"

"Why, yes," he said, strolling forward and circling her critically, as if she were a brood mare he was contemplating buying. "You know what they say:

156

Mommy and Daddy and baby make three. Unless you visited a sperm bank in order to have a child, in which case, of course, the donor wouldn't be included in the equation.''

''I didn't visit a sperm bank,'' she said faintly, her skin prickling under his unremitting scrutiny.

He took another leisurely turn around her, came to a stop barely six inches in front of her and, rocking back and forth on the balls of his feet, continued to spear her with his gaze.

Mesmerized, she stared back, registering the changes in him. Despite the heavy Aran sweater he wore, she could see that he'd lost weight and looked like a man on the brink of exhaustion. His faded tan spoke of too many hours spent indoors, and the dark circles under his eyes, which once had earmarked him as an overworked intern at the beck and call of more senior staff, were back and more pronounced than ever.

Suddenly, he reached out and plucked from her hand the print-out of her ultrasound, which showed her baby curled up in her womb with one hand tucked sweetly under its chin. ''My goodness, Olivia,'' he said, his tone still excruciatingly polite as his glance charted the fuzzy image on the paper, ''I'm no obstetrician but I'd say from looking at this that you're well into your second trimester. You didn't waste much time taking a new lover once I was out of the picture, did you?''

He was toying with her, of course; baiting her and enjoying watching her squirm. Clearly someone had informed him about the baby and he'd leapt to the right conclusion regarding its paternity. ''There was no other lover and you know it,'' she said wearily. ''This is your child I'm carrying, Grant.''

''Is it indeed? And when were you planning on sharing the news with me, dear?''

He'd never called her ''dear'' in his life. She hoped he never would again; he'd cloaked the word in such a wealth of contempt. ''I—''

His eyes bored into her, cold blue steel cutting clean through to her soul. ''Spare me your lies, Olivia. The answer is, never.''

''No!'' she said. ''That's not true. I would have told you, eventually. I would never deprive a child from knowing his father.''

He took her chin between his thumb and forefinger and tilted her face up to his. ''You say that with such convincing sincerity. Anyone who didn't know you would swallow your story wholesale. Hell, I'm almost ready to believe you myself, except I know how good you are at leading people on. Letting them think you're on their side. Preying on their susceptibilities to get your own way.''

He jerked away from her as if he'd found himself touching filth, and swung back to the window. ''I have to hand it to you, dear. Your timing was impeccable.''

''Timing? You think I planned to get pregnant?''

''Let's just say you orchestrated things to cash in on the possibility. You're a well-informed woman, Olivia. You know how the female body works. You know when ovulation occurs. Your moving little outburst of helpless tears at the Sunflower Ball was a stroke of brilliance. Not many men cope well with that kind of stunt, you know? But of course you know! It was all part of your master plan, just like the dress that practically fell off your beautiful body without my having to lift a finger, and you with barely a stitch on underneath, just when you were at your most fertile and there wasn't a condom in sight.''

''Do you really think I'm capable of that kind of manipulation?'' she asked, dazed. ''Is that the kind of woman that comes to mind when you think of me?''

''No,'' he said. ''When I'm foolish enough to allow myself to think of you at all, I skip the ugly parts and go back to the time when I was a green, know-it-all intern and a young woman walked into a patient's room at Springdale General. She was doling out books from the portable library cart and I was supposed to be checking the patient's blood pressure—except it was mine that soared at the sight of this angel-faced creature who looked as if she'd just stepped from the pages of a kid's book of fairy tales.''

''Oh, Grant!'' she whispered, her heart so full and hurting she could scarcely breathe. ''Please don't do this!''

He carried on anyway. ''Was she beautiful, you ask? You bet! Innocent? In spades! Yet there was a sensuality about her made all the more appealing because she wasn't even aware of it. I'd known my share of women, some older than I, some younger, but none quite like her. Do you want me to tell you what I felt when I looked at her?''

''No,'' Olivia quavered, because the pain so clearly tearing through his voice was ravaging her, too.

He turned and looked at her across the width of the room, his features trapped in a bright swath of sunlight that revealed the raw emotion he was fighting so hard to contain. ''She wore her long, dark blonde hair loose and it was all I could do not to run my fingers through it. As for her eyes—well, there ought to be a law about a woman walking around with weapons so lethal they'd persuade a man to sell his soul! Then there was the small matter of her mouth— 'luscious' is the word that comes to mind.''

He balled his fist and thumped it lightly against the wooden window frame. ''I'd keep going if it weren't that words, at least those at my command, don't begin to do her justice. The best analogy I can come up with is to think of a summer-ripe, sun-kissed peach and imagine sinking my teeth into it and having my mouth filled with bursting flavor. Juice with a hint of wine, syrup touched with delicate, lemony tartness. A beguiling contradiction in terms, wouldn't you say, and impossible to forget?''

''But why would you hang on to memories of someone you frequently found tiresomely immature?'' Olivia asked, stunned by the repressed passion in his voice.

''Because it's preferable to facing what you are today: a woman who'd deliberately withhold from me knowledge that I've fathered a child. If I dwell too long on that fact, I tend to start thinking in terms of custody suits, and I don't much like the kind of guy that makes me.''

She thought she was going to faint. ''Is that why you came back? To challenge my right to bring up this baby?''

''No,'' he said coldly. ''To protect my right to determine how you go about doing it.''

''How dare you come here and threaten me like this?'' she flung at him, memories different from his stirring her to retaliate. "I'm not the one who was glad when my last pregnancy ended in miscarriage."

"I've already admitted my attitude then left something to be desired."

"*Something to be desired?* You have a very selective memory when it comes to dredging up your past sins, Grant Madison! I distinctly recall the words you flung at me the day I came home and told you we were going to have a baby. 'We can't handle this right now,' you said. 'Our marriage is under enough strain already. The last thing we need is adding a kid to the mix.' That's all he was to you: a 'kid' who'd tie you down to one place when what you wanted was the freedom to wander wherever adventure beckoned."

She placed her hands protectively over the swell of her pregnancy. "And you wonder why I didn't rush to tell you about this little one? Frankly, he'd be better off not knowing you existed than be saddled with an unwilling, resentful father."

"Is that why you moved back home, Olivia?" Grant said coldly. "To make it more convenient for Grand-daddy Dearest to take my place?"

"No," she said, "although it doesn't surprise me that that's the conclusion you'd jump to. I really wonder at your own motives, that you're so ready to question everyone else's. For example, you knew I wasn't on the pill when we met again last summer, so why didn't *you* take responsibility for contraception the night of the Sunflower Ball, the way you did every time after that when we were together? Why is it all my fault that we've made another baby? Because it doesn't matter who takes the blame as long as it doesn't land on you? Does it help you justify your present rotten behavior by pretending I dragged you, kicking and screaming, into my bed, and forced you against your will to impregnate me? Well, I've got news for you, *Doctor*! That's not how it works with men. Only women can fake it!''

''You do a lot of that, do you?'' he cut in silkily. ''Faking it, I mean?''

She gasped as if he'd struck her. ''How can you even think such a thing?'' she cried, tears of rage stinging her eyes. ''How can you take the one part of our relationship that was always perfect, no matter what else was going wrong, and tarnish it with your…your…?''

He almost looked ashamed. ''I don't know. So help me, you bring out the worst in me every time. I do and say the damnedest things when I'm around you. But you're right. Sex was always good between us and I was out of line to accuse you like that.''

''Well, it's too late because the damage is done!'' She slapped at the conciliatory hand he extended, and, as if just touching him had let loose a flood of pent-up fury, kept on flailing at him—at his arms, his shoulders, anywhere she could land a passing blow. ''I was right to leave you last September. I was right to try to forget I ever met you. I wish I never had. You break everything you touch! Well, you're not going to break me, not this time. I won't let you do that to me ever again.''

''Calm down, for Pete's sake!'' he ordered, and, when she continued to berate him, caught her to him in a bone-crushing hold. ''Listen to me! Getting upset like this isn't good for you or the baby.''

''As if you care about either one of us! You probably hope I miscarry this time as well!''

He went suddenly still, then very gently put her

from him. "If I've ever given you the impression that I'd wish that on any mother or her child, then it's small wonder we couldn't make a go of things the second time around. The miracle is that you even bothered to try. I might not have honored my wedding vows as well as I should have, but I can promise you I'd sooner die than betray my Hippocratic oath."

She wished she dared believe him. But his being there, the angst of seeing him, of fighting him, on top of everything else she was trying to cope with, left her too drained and confused to know what to think. She felt almost ill. "Please leave," she said. "I can't deal with any more of this right now."

"Sending me away isn't going to change the fact that we made this child together, Olivia, or that I fully intend sharing the responsibility in raising him. I didn't just happen to show up in Springdale by accident, you know. I'm interviewing for a job at the hospital with the intent of making a permanent move here so that I can be on hand to play a major role in our son or daughter's life."

He was coming back, to a town he'd always rather despised, just because of her and their baby? She grasped the back of a chair and collapsed like a strand of limp spaghetti on the arm, light-headed with a hope made all the more absurd by the fact that his chief objective appeared to be protecting his rights as a father rather than trying yet again to fix what was broken between them.

He studied her with some concern. "You look completely washed out. Is there something wrong—something about the pregnancy that you're not telling me?"

"Beyond the fact that stress isn't the best medicine

for anyone, regardless of whether or not she's expecting, you mean?'' she said, waving him away when he approached. She'd fall apart if he tried to touch her again. Even at a distance, the soap and aftershave scent of him, his blue-eyed candor, the sexy curve of his mouth which not even anger could diminish, reached out to ensnare her and left her quivering for him. ''No. I just need to sit down for a while. I tire very easily these days.''

''Then I'll leave and let you get some rest. But I'll be back because, like it or not, we're in this together and we have to resolve how we're going to deal with it.'' He cleared his throat, and if she hadn't known him incapable of such human weakness she'd have thought he was nervous. ''Would you consider having dinner with me tonight? If that country inn you used to like so much—you know the one I mean, about twenty-five miles east of town? What was it called?''

''The Sherlow.''

''Yeah, that's it. If it's still in business—''

''It is.''

''Okay. We'll drive out there and just talk things over while we enjoy a good meal. Try to act like rational human beings, for a change, instead of going for each other's jugular. What do you say, Olivia?''

He could be the most persuasive man ever created when he put his mind to it. He knew just the right tone of voice to use, just the right look to weaken her resolve. But was she wise to let him seduce her into compliance again so easily? Could she go with him again to that lovely old lodge, with its steep, gabled roof and tall chimneys and paned windows, and not be swamped by a slew of memories best left undisturbed? Of firelight flickering on paneled walls, and silver gleaming in the glow of candles set in crystal holders on linen tablecloths starched to a fare-thee-well, and a spindled balustrade disappearing into the shadows of an upper floor?

Could she remain focused on the here and now, and not allow her thoughts to drift back to another night when they'd sat across from each other in that elegant, old-world dining room, and ended up in a four-poster bed in a room tucked under the eaves? Was it possible he didn't even remember that that was where they'd conceived their first child?

She sagged against the back of the chair. "I'm not sure I'm up to it today, Grant."

"Putting it off until tomorrow isn't going to accomplish anything. We're going to have to arrive at some sort of understanding, sooner or later."

"All *right*!" She heaved a sigh, too worn down by other matters that had nothing to do with him, their past, or their baby, and which she could never expect him to appreciate. She didn't have the energy to go toe to toe with him on anything else. There were bigger battles to be fought. "Have it your way. We'll go to dinner."

Gracious in victory, he pressed her shoulder reassuringly. "You won't regret it. I'll pick you up at seven."

He'd asked them at the hospital to give him until Monday to decide if he wanted the position, but he knew he might as well ink the deal right away and have done with it. Not that there was anything wrong with what he'd been offered; the job had all the prestige, perks and challenge he could ask for.

In fact, in order to remain close to Olivia, he'd have

settled for far less than they'd been willing to give. The visible evidence of her pregnancy had affected him more than he'd anticipated and stirred him to strange longings.

As he drove away from Whitfield House, it wasn't the snow piled high beside the curb, or the bare branches of the trees etched against the brilliant blue sky that caught his attention. His vision was turned inward, on a boy racing across a grassy field with a ball and calling him "Dad". Or perhaps a girl who was a carbon copy of her mother, looking at him as if she thought he was God and could stop the earth from spinning if he chose.

The big flaw in the picture was the notion of his being a sometime-parent, the guy who showed up on Saturday and spent a wad of money to make up for the fact that Sam Whitfield filled his shoes the rest of the time.

He didn't think he could stomach that. When Olivia had become pregnant the first time, it had been all he could do not to hurl at her father's confident assumption that *he'd* be the guiding influence in the child's upbringing. His grandchild was going to *have* this, *do* that, *be* the other.

If he hadn't realized it before, Grant had known then that the only chance he and Olivia stood of making their marriage work was for him to take her as far away as possible from Springdale and her father. To that end, he'd signed a two-year contract to work up north within the month.

When Olivia and Sam had found out, they'd gone ballistic. The tears, the threats, the cold, unforgiving rage: caught between them, he'd been at his wits' end. Money had been scarce, but he'd been on solid ground professionally and willing to play the hand he'd been dealt, given a bit of emotional support from his wife.

But she hadn't had it in her, not then. When he'd had the chance to attend an important medical conference in Chicago later that spring, she'd refused to go with him, claiming pregnancy left her too enervated to cope with the journey.

So he'd gone alone—in a huff, he had to admit. And she'd miscarried while he was away, with dear old Dad right there on the scene, stoking the fires of resentment and urging her to pack in a marriage which had been a mistake from the first.

Things weren't much more promising now. He and Olivia were about as far apart as a couple could get and still be on the same planet. About the only thing they agreed on was the time of day. If they didn't want their child paying a terrible price, they were both going to have to make changes. He was willing to try. Willing to do whatever it took. The question remained, was she?

"One thing at a time, buddy," he muttered, swinging into the hospital parking lot. "Take care of business here, then find a place to live. Maybe when she sees you're in this for the long haul, she'll be inclined to view you more favorably."

But the physical impact of seeing her again had affected him in ways he hadn't counted on. In some ways, she was even lovelier in pregnancy: more lushly rounded, more womanly, if that was possible. He had wanted to touch her intimately. To test the fullness of her breasts in the palm of his hand and kiss their delicate tracery of veins. To press his ear to her belly and listen to his child, to speak to him.

In others, she looked almost transparently frail. By her own admission, she was over-tired and over-stressed. Not a good combination for a woman with a history of miscarriage.

Gradually, the anger which had fueled him all the way from Vancouver to Springdale had channeled its energy to a different focus, one geared toward reconciliation instead of confrontation, toward armistice instead of aggression. He'd begun to rethink his options.

Which was why, rather than looking at apartments streamlined to cater to bachelor tastes as he'd originally planned, he found himself seeking out houses intended for families. Places with safe, fenced gardens and extra bedrooms, and kitchens designed with a woman in mind. And another solution—some might say the obvious and only solution—began to take shape in his mind.

Could they do it? Were the stakes high enough to make it worth their taking another stab at marriage?

The clarity of his own conviction lifted the fog of uncertainty which had plagued him for days. Suddenly, more than anything, he wanted to try.

There'd be no point in blathering on about love, of course. That wasn't likely to cut any ice with her, in view of the way he'd treated her recently, so he'd have to take a different tack. *Think of the baby,* he'd say. *He deserves to have both parents and shouldn't have to pay for our mistakes. We'll make it work for his sake.*

If she turned him down, as seemed likely, he'd keep badgering her until she said yes. Not just because no kid of his was going to be labeled a bastard, or left to believe his old man hadn't cared enough about him to put his interests first, but because she needed a husband as much as their child needed a father.

If she'd gone running back home to find emotional and physical support, old Sam was falling down on the job and it was time for someone else to take over. The way Grant saw it, he was perfectly qualified to be that someone.

There were no messages waiting when he checked in at his room at The Ambassador, which was a good sign. At least she hadn't backed out of their dinner plans. He phoned for a reservation at The Sherlow, then poured himself a Scotch, figuring he had time to rehearse how he was going to propose before he showered and shaved and went to collect her.

Traffic was slow as he crossed the bridge and turned up the curving hill that led to the part of town where Whitfield House and all the other old-money estates were located. Although the road had been plowed, it had been reduced to one lane each way, and some of the cars trying to make the grade were finding it tough going on the icy surface.

It didn't help matters when an ambulance came racing down the other way, with lights flashing and sirens screaming. In line with everyone else, Grant pulled as far over to the side as he could get, to allow it to pass, then spent another fifteen minutes giving the car in front a push from behind to get it moving again. He was almost twenty minutes late arriving at the house.

"Evening, Edward," he said, when the butler answered the door. "I'm here to pick up Miss Olivia."

The old man looked shaken. "Oh, sir, she's not here."

For a minute, Grant wondered if they'd arranged to meet at the inn. Had he misunderstood? Had she? "What do you mean, she isn't here? Where is she?"

"At the hospital. The ambulance left not long ago. You must have—"

He didn't wait for the butler to finish. There was no point. He could hear nothing over the pounding of his heart and the remembered wail of the sirens fading in the night. The only thought hammering in his mind was that the noise they made inside an ambulance was so deafening that they were used only when absolutely necesasry. In other words, in cases of extreme urgency.

He raced back to his car, swung it around in a skidding circle, and headed back the way he'd come, scarcely aware that he kept repeating, "Oh, please God, no, not again!"

Scarcely aware that, for the first time in his life, he was praying.

It was his fault. He'd done it. Hounding her, insulting her, threatening her. *You break everything you touch,* she'd said, and she was right. But not this, please God! He was a doctor, for pity's sake! To have his own child's blood on his hands, to have jeopardized the safety and well-being of the only woman he'd ever love, to have broken her heart and her spirit yet again…!

Because she was Sam Whitfield's daughter, they found her an empty room where she could wait. They brought her hot tea and forms to fill and told her not to worry, that they were doing everything they could for him but that it might take some time, and unfortunately they couldn't spare anyone to sit with her and keep her company. Saturday nights were the busiest in ER, and it was worse that night because of the road conditions. More accidents than usual, they said.

Their words and faces ran together, like raindrops sheeting down a window and washing away everything but the one fact she couldn't escape: it was her fault. She shouldn't have told him Grant was back in town and that they were going out for dinner. He wasn't strong enough to cope with anything other than getting through each day. He never would be again. Just making it downstairs was an ordeal. He was dying and he knew it. All he wanted was to live long enough to see his grandchild.

Outside the room, rubber-soled shoes squeaked faintly down the hall, equipment rattled, gurneys swished by. The elevator next door pinged at regular intervals.

A sudden commotion arose. She heard voices, the muted, soothing tones of nurses drowned out by one of masculine authority, followed by a sound she recognized, one that struck fear in the hearts of people she'd tried to comfort as they'd waited for news on their loved ones: the repeated beep-beep-beep of the Code Blue alarm used in the ER.

The very atmosphere seemed to hang in fearful suspension. She wanted to stand up, to rush to the cubicle where they were trying to stabilize her father. But she might have been cast in stone. While her mind raced frantically, her limbs remained paralyzed.

And then the door burst open and Grant was there, wild-eyed and haggard, striding toward her and co-

cooning her in his arms and brokenly murmuring her name.

Oh, the news must be bad, if even he was distressed!

The knowledge unspooled in her head and wove in dizzying circles before her eyes. She clutched at Grant, for anything that might anchor her. But a mist was swirling around her and she was suffocating in it. And he was disappearing into it. Beyond her reach, when she needed him most, just as always....

CHAPTER ELEVEN

HIS voice penetrated the darkness, deep and soothing and tender, drawing her back to the light. "Open your eyes, Liv," he crooned.

She did, and found him sitting beside her on the couch.

"That's better." He stroked the hair from her forehead and smiled down at her. "The next time you faint, try to give me a bit more warning, okay? Taking a nose-dive from across the room is guaranteed to grab a guy's attention, but it plays havoc with his nerves."

"You don't have any nerves," she said fuzzily. "You're the original iron man."

"Not me, sweetheart. Not any more. You just knocked the last of that out of me."

The way his smile faded away brought a knot of fear to her throat. She slid both hands over her abdomen, a gesture she'd repeated often in recent weeks, and felt a surge of gratitude at the familiar bulge located exactly where it was supposed to be.

"Yes, he's still in there cooking," Grant said, reaching over to the end table beside the couch and picking up a sort of microphone with an electric cord attached. "This is a Doppler, sweetheart. It works like a radio transmitter, picking up the sound of an unborn baby's heartbeat. May I?"

He gestured at her stomach, and she, not realizing

all that was involved, and in desperate need of reassurance, nodded permission.

Before she knew it, he'd raised her dress and slid down her underpants just far enough to expose her belly. Had done it so deftly and professionally that her embarrassment at his seeing her revealed in all her bloated glory seemed ludicrous.

"There," he said, rolling the instrument over the taut slope of her abdomen and coming to a stop about an inch below her navel. "Hear that?"

She did, but the energetically rapid little beat reminded her of another heart, so damaged it was close to wearing out. "My father," she whispered, pushing aside the Doppler and struggling to sit up. "I heard the Code Blue alarm. Is he—?"

"It wasn't for Sam, sweetheart," Grant said calmly. "At last report, he was holding his own."

But she saw the guarded expression in his eyes. "There's something you're not telling me. Let me up. I want to see him for myself."

"No." He pressed her back down on the couch. "They won't let you see him, not yet. You'd just be in the way and there's nothing you can do that isn't already being done, so please try to stay calm. Put yourself and the baby first, for a change."

"You don't really believe he's all that seriously ill, do you?" she said bitterly. "You think I'm making a lot of fuss about nothing again."

"Oh, sweetheart, no!" He lifted her hands and kissed them one at a time, then, with a depth of feeling he seldom allowed himself, mumbled, "I'm so ashamed, Olivia. I've been wrong about so many things. If only I'd realized…"

He shook his head, disgust and despair mirrored in

every line of his face. "Why didn't you tell me that the reason you moved back to your dad's house is that you've being acting as his nursemaid for the last four months?"

"Would you have believed me, if I had?"

"Yes."

"The way you did in Lake Louise, when I tried to tell you he wasn't well?"

He studied her for a moment, then had the grace to lower his gaze. "Okay, I deserved that. But I'm listening now, and I want to help. I won't lie to you. Sam's in pretty rough shape. If he makes it through the next couple of days, his chances are good, but the road to recovery's going to be long and hard. Lean on me, sweetheart, please. You've carried this burden alone for long enough."

"Someone has to look out for him."

"And someone will. We all will. I'll arrange round-the-clock nursing care, if that's what he needs. I'll make it my personal business to see that he receives the best possible care. I'll consult with his doctors on every step of his treatment."

"Why, Grant? Because you feel guilty?"

"Yes, damn it! And because I've just gone through a scare that's taken ten years off my life." He prowled the room restlessly, then dropped to his heels beside her. "I thought you were the one they'd brought in to Emergency, Liv. I thought you were miscarrying again and that it was my fault."

"How could it have been?" she said, pity for him mingling with anxiety for her father.

"Because I saw how worn out you were this morning, and I kept pressuring you anyway. I'm supposed to be a doctor, for pity's sake! I should have known better. I *did* know better. But did I let that stop me from badgering you?'' He lifted her hands and pressed an anguished kiss to her knuckles. ''When Edward told me…and I thought…I was so afraid, Liv. For you and for the baby.''

''I didn't think anything could frighten you.''

He gave a small embarrassed laugh. ''If you'd seen the state I was in earlier, you'd change your mind! I must have violated every traffic regulation in the book racing to get here, and I shudder to think of the reputation I've earned with the ER staff because of the way I acted when I arrived.''

''I'm glad you're with me, Grant,'' she said, touching his cheek with the back of her hand. ''It makes the waiting easier.''

''I want to be with you all the time,'' he said urgently. ''Liv, I want us to get married, as soon as possible. It'll work out this time, I promise. Things'll be different. I'll *make* them different.''

They were the words she'd longed to hear, but not like this, inspired by remorse and fear. ''No,'' she said. ''Despite his faults, and regardless of what you think of him, I'm all the family my father has. In his own way, he loves me and has always stood by me. Now it's my turn to stand by him.''

''Well, I love you, too!'' Grant exclaimed, but he robbed the moment of any magic it might have held by spitting out the declaration as if the very taste of it repelled him.

''And you wish you didn't,'' she said.

He glowered at her. ''Because it's easier not caring! But I can't seem to help myself. You're a part of me and you always will be, and now, with a baby on the way, it's time I faced up to the fact.''

That he sounded more like a man facing up to an inevitable but undesirable fate, rather than one committed to love and marriage, saddened her unbearably. It seemed that the best they could ever achieve was to come within kissing distance of true happiness. At the last, it always eluded them.

"I realize this is hardly the time or place to start planning a future together," he went on, reading the doubt she knew was written all over her face, "but I'm speaking from my heart, Olivia, when I say that our getting married is in everyone's best interests."

"I think it needs to be more than that, Grant. Even marriages of convenience need a smattering of romance to see them over the rough spots."

"I think we could do better than just a smattering," he said, sitting beside her again and grasping her hands. "I think, given half a chance, we could light up the sky like a rocket."

"Perhaps we could, but if you really care as much as you claim, you won't keep pressing the issue now. Neither of us should be making life-altering decisions at a time like this." She pushed herself upright, glad to discover that her legs weren't about to buckle under her, and headed for the door. "I don't want a husband by default, and I know from bitter experience that the last thing you want is a clinging wife who can't cope with her own problems."

"People change, Olivia," he said. "I have, and I'll prove it to you."

Instead of answering him, she opened the door and walked out of the room.

"Where do you think you're going?" he said, catching up with her at the elevator.

She turned her lovely eyes on him. The weariness

he saw in them made him bleed inside. "Where do you think? I'm going to find my father."

"No," he said, barring her way. This was his area of expertise, and he knew too well the kind of scene she might walk in on if he let her go up to CCU. Watching a body jerk off a bed in response to the electric paddles wasn't a pretty sight, even for hardened professionals. The choking, the vomit, the absolute indignity of a human being *in extremis* was tough to take, and from all he'd heard Sam was likely to be suffering them all. It was better that she not see him. "Wait here and let me go instead. I'll give you a report, I promise."

"No," she said. "How do I know that you'll tell me the truth?"

"Because whatever else my sins, I've never lied to you, Olivia, and I'm not about to start now. Come up to CCU with me if you wish, but please wait outside until I've had a chance to see how he's doing."

He took her shrug to mean assent, and guided her into the elevator. Visiting hours were long over on the Critical Care floor, and the hall was deserted as he made his way toward the Cardiac Unit and left her in the waiting area.

Sam was in the first bay, but if the nurse in charge hadn't pointed him out, Grant doubted he'd have recognized him. The figure in the bed was a shadow of the heavy-set man he'd last seen. Only his years of training and experience enabled Grant to maintain his composure as he drew up a stool and faced his old nemesis.

Although he wouldn't have been proud to admit it, he'd have expected the best he could drum up in the way of emotion would be professional pity. Yet, for reasons that completely defied explanation, he was filled with inexpressible personal sadness at the sight of the indomitable old bulldog reduced to such straits.

"Well, Sam," he said quietly. "So it's come to this, has it? You're going to check out before my son is born because you can't stand the thought that he might look like me."

"I'm not...checking out," Sam gasped. "Not until you and Olivia straighten out the...mess you've made of things. I'm not like you, Grant Madison. I don't walk away and...leave a job half done."

"If I didn't know better, I'd think you wanted to see us get back together, Sam," he said, eyeing the monitor over the bed and feeling cautiously pleased at what he saw. The old guy was hanging tough. He wouldn't give in without a fight.

A grimace which might have been a smile touched Sam's mouth. "Might not be such a...bad thing. Somebody's got to whip you into shape before that baby arrives."

Grant bent low and looked directly into his former father-in-law's eyes. "I agree. That's why I just proposed to Olivia. Trouble is, I've run into a snag. She turned me down because she doesn't think you and I can learn to get along. So cancel the one-way ticket out of here, you old buzzard, because I'm not about to have you screw up my plans by dying on me."

This time, a definite laugh wheezed out. "Hell, Madison, I wouldn't...give you the pleasure!"

"That's good," Grant said, floored to find himself on the brink of tears. "Because every kid deserves a grandfather, and there aren't any left on my side of the family. You've got two pairs of shoes to fill, Sam, and I intend to make sure you're up to the job. So chew on that while I go get your daughter. She wants to give her old man a kiss and remind him that she loves him. But I'll be back in the morning, and I'm leaving orders at the desk to call me if you need me during the night.''

"You take care of Olivia," Sam said. "They've got nurses here to look after me."

There were buds on the maple trees before her father was ready to come home again, and she knew she'd never have survived the ordeal of watching him struggle back to health if it hadn't been for Grant.

Whenever he'd been able to, he'd driven her to the hospital. He'd made himself available to consult on every aspect of Sam's treatment and recovery. He'd anticipated her every need, catered to her every whim. He'd held her hand and massaged her shoulders and kissed her cheek. But after that terrible night, when she'd thought her father was surely going to die, he'd honored her wishes and never again broached the subject of marriage.

It was as if, by the time the immediate crisis was past, he'd shelved any idea of becoming her husband again and settled for the friendship he'd once insisted was the cornerstone of any relationship.

"Sam needs a bedroom on the ground floor," he'd said, a couple of weeks before her father was released from the hospital, and had immediately taken charge of making the change, bringing in contractors and plumbers to convert the library wing into a private suite with an extra room for a live-in nurse.

He'd taken her out to dinner sometimes, and sometimes brought meals to the house, courtesy of Ingrid from the deli. One time, when he'd been tied up with a particularly difficult case at the hospital, he'd actually called on Henry to make sure she didn't miss an appointment with her obstetrician.

I don't want Henry, she'd felt like telling him. *I want you. Stop being so nice and start making demands on me again.*

She thought perhaps it was pregnancy that left her aching for him. "Some women are like that, from what I've read," Bethany snickered, when she confided in her. "They just can't get enough sex. Others don't want anything to do with it. If I were you, I'd just jump his bones one night and get it over with. I'm sure he'd be willing to accommodate you."

If only she dared! But there was a thin wall of reserve between them that kept him at a distance.

"Will you be here tomorrow when my dad comes home?" she asked him, the Tuesday before the big day.

"I don't think so," he said. "He'll be pretty tired and won't be up to visitors."

"You're more than a visitor, Grant, and I think he'd like to see you. He's become quite dependent on you, in case you haven't noticed."

"That often happens to patients who've been through a bad time in hospital. Let's give him a few days to adjust to being home again."

"Does that mean I won't be seeing you, either?" she asked in a small voice.

He patted her stomach. "I'll keep in touch, Olivia, don't worry."

But only because of the baby, she thought resentfully.

The rest of the week went by, and, although he phoned regularly to see how her father was coping, he didn't once come to the house. Finally, she'd had enough. She called him at the hospital and put it to him point-blank. "Are you avoiding me, Grant?"

"Of course not," he said equably.

"Good. Then come for dinner on Saturday. I miss you."

"Will your father be joining us?"

"No," she said. "Not if you don't want him to."

"But I do. In fact, I insist on it."

She should have been delighted at his changed attitude. Instead, she was quite put out.

She spent Saturday morning at the hairdresser's, met Bethany for lunch, then stopped by the deli to pick up the items Ingrid had prepared for that evening. Edward, who usually took care of the cooking as well as just about everything else around Whitfield House, had enough to do competing with the nurse over which of them had first dibs on attending to her father's needs.

Later in the afternoon, she took a nap, then spent another hour taking a leisurely bath. She chose a maternity dress Grant hadn't seen before, a royal blue wool-silk blend cut along empire lines, with a boat-shaped neck and three-quarter sleeves trimmed in matching satin ribbon. Last, before she went down to wait for him to arrive, she hung a thin gold chain around her neck, tucked it inside the top of her dress, and wore a pearl choker on top to hide it.

He came early, and brought two bottles of non-alcoholic sparkling white wine. "This stuff might not fool a connoisseur like you, Sam, but it looks and tastes enough like champagne to celebrate your homecoming in some sort of style," he said, pecking Olivia on the cheek in passing and handing her father a glass. "Here's to your recovery and a renewed lease on life."

"Here's to a healthy grandchild," her father said. "Can't wait to hold the little tyke on my lap. Got any names in mind for him?"

Grant laughed. "Not Sam, if that's what you're hoping, and not Grant."

"Especially not if she's a girl," Olivia said snippily, beginning to think she might as well be invisible for all the notice they were taking of her. "And, if you're both done, I'd like to propose a toast."

She swallowed, gripped by a bout of nervous apprehension now that the moment was upon her, then plunged on, "Actually, I'd like to propose. Grant, in January you asked me to marry you, and I couldn't give you an answer at the time. You don't seem inclined to repeat the offer, so now I'm asking you. Are you still willing to make an honest woman of me, or has the idea grown stale?"

"Gee," he said, almost choking on his ersatz champagne. "You've sort of taken me by surprise, sweet face. I didn't bring a ring."

"That's all right, I came prepared." She fished the gold chain out from beneath the pearl choker and dangled it in front of him to show off the diamond solitaire suspended from it. "I still have the original here, and if it's all the same to you, I'd just as soon stick with it the second time around."

He rolled his eyes. "And you once accused me of not being romantic!"

"I happen to think some things are worth saving," she said. "This ring is one of them, and you and I as a couple are another. So what do you say, Grant Madison?"

"She's asking you to put your money where your mouth is," her father cackled.

"Please don't turn this into a sitcom, Dad," she said severely. "Well, Grant? Are you going to sit there all night like a stuffed dummy, or what?"

"Don't you think we should discuss it first, Olivia? There are a few things that need to be settled."

"Such as what?" she said, feeling like a perfect fool. She'd offered him her heart and seemed in danger of having it handed back to her with a polite *No, thanks!*

"Well, the last time I brought up the question of marriage, you weren't at all sure the experiment was worth repeating. What changed your mind?"

"You did," she said. "If I wanted proof that you really care about me, you've given it to me, every day for the last twelve weeks or more. I don't want to bring up this baby alone, Grant. I want him to know firsthand what a fine daddy he has. And I don't think I can bear having to beg like this much longer, so if you're not interested, just say so."

He leaned one elbow on the arm of his chair and rested his chin on his fist. "Hmm," he said, slewing a sly glance her father's way. "And where do you propose we set up house?"

"Well, my old place is very comfortable, and it does have three bedrooms. I know how you feel about taking anything from my father, but if you could see your way clear to—"

"Uh-uh!" He shook his head. "I'm afraid I wouldn't find that at all acceptable."

She could have wept with frustrated disappointment. "So all your fine talk of being willing to change stops short when it comes to your making a few concessions, does it? Even though my father's welcomed you into his house and made it clear he no longer holds a grudge, you're determined to hang on to old resentments?''

"Did I say that?'' He turned to her father, eyebrows raised dramatically. "Did I, Sam?''

"You haven't much of a chance to say anything, if you ask me,'' her father replied, holding up his glass and inspecting the narrow ribbons of bubbles rising to the surface of its pale gold contents. "Olivia's doing most of the talking, and putting her foot in her mouth with damn near every word. Maybe you should tell her what you've got up your sleeve, and put her out of her misery.''

"Maybe you're right.'' He came to her, removed the glass from her hand and dropped down on one knee before her. "When you propose, sweet face, this is how you're supposed to go about it.''

His face was on a level with her bulging middle. He patted it as if it were an overweight dog begging for attention. "However, in light of the fact that you're only six weeks away from delivery, I'm willing to be the one to grovel. Yes, I'll marry you, Olivia, but the gatehouse is out of the question because I've already made other living arrangements. There are too many empty rooms in this house which need to be filled, and, since I'm hoping to convince you not to stop at one child, it makes more sense for us to live here.''

She couldn't be hearing right. "With my *father*?''

"Well, I wasn't planning on evicting him, if that's what you think! He still holds title to the place, after all.''

"But you and he disagree about so many things. It would never work."

"We think it will. It's taken us a while, but we've finally come to realize we're both on the same side where you're concerned, my love. We want to see you happy. And it's not as if we're going to be falling all over each other every time we turn around."

"You might as well stop fighting him, Olivia," her father said. "When a man makes up his mind, there's not much a woman can do to change it."

"Shut up, Sam, before you screw things up," Grant said.

Amazingly, her father did.

Grant stood up and held her hands securely in his. "So what do you say, Liv?"

She shook her head, too overcome to speak.

Misinterpreting her silence for doubt, he squeezed her fingers. "No guts, no glory, sweet face, remember?"

"I know," she wailed, the tears dribbling down her face and taking half her make-up with them.

"You aren't supposed to make her cry, Grant Madison," her father said. "That wasn't part of the deal."

"I'm not," he said. "She's just having one of those hormonal showers that come with pregnancy. Relax, old man, your daughter's safe with me."

And she knew that she was. "Let's do it," she said, smiling through the tears.

They were married two weeks later, on a fine spring day full of sun and early daffodils. Because she knew by then that the baby was a girl, Olivia wore pink, with a wide-brimmed hat to match, and carried a bouquet of cream roses. Grant wore a pale gray suit and tie, a white shirt, and an I-can't-wait-to-get-to-the-honeymoon-part-of-this-shindig look in his eye.

Her father wore a grin that wouldn't go away.

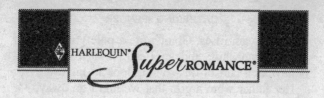

HARLEQUIN *Super*ROMANCE®

...there's more to the story!

Superromance.
A *big* satisfying read about unforgettable
characters. Each month we offer *six* very different
stories that range from family drama to adventure
and mystery, from highly emotional stories to
romantic comedies—and much more! Stories
about people you'll believe in and care about.
Stories too compelling to put down....

Our authors are among today's *best* romance
writers. You'll find familiar names and talented
newcomers. Many of them are award winners—
and you'll see why!

If you want the biggest and best
in romance fiction, you'll get it
from Superromance!

Emotional, Exciting, Unexpected...

HARLEQUIN®
*M*akes any time special®

Visit us at www.eHarlequin.com

HARLEQUIN®
INTRIGUE

WE'LL LEAVE YOU BREATHLESS!

If you've been looking for thrilling tales of
contemporary passion and sensuous love stories
with taut, edge-of-the-seat suspense—then
you'll love Harlequin Intrigue!

Every month, you'll meet four new heroes
who are guaranteed to make your spine tingle
and your pulse pound. With them you'll enter
into the exciting world of Harlequin Intrigue—
where your life is on the line
and so is your heart!

THAT'S INTRIGUE—
ROMANTIC SUSPENSE
AT ITS BEST!

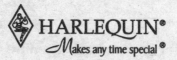

HARLEQUIN®
Makes any time special ®

SILHOUETTE *Romance™*

Escape to a place where a kiss is still a kiss...
Feel the breathless connection...
Fall in love as though it were
the very first time...
Experience the power of love!

Come to where favorite authors——such as
Diana Palmer, Stella Bagwell,
Marie Ferrarella and many more——
deliver heart-warming romance and genuine
emotion, time after time after time....

Silhouette Romance——
stories straight from the heart!

Silhouette®
Where love comes alive™